Critter Capers

CRITTER CAPERS

Tales from the Dogcatcher who captures your heart

Lee Wittek

Cover Story: Misty, the mixed breed Australian Shepherd puppy that graces the cover was adopted from the Carson City, Nevada Animal Shelter in 1987. She continued to delight all met her until she left this earthly plane in 2002.

Published by BBM Press, P. O. Box 2512, Carson City NV 89702

Editor:	Maggie Mitchell
Page designer:	Syd Brown
Typographer:	Syd Brown

BBM Press
P. O. Box 2512 • Carson City NV 89702
Phone/Fax: (775) 883-4628
For easy ordering call 1-800-BOOKLOG

ISBN 0-972287-21-3

Printed in the United States of America

1 2 3 4 5 6 7 8 9 – BM – 07 06 05 04 03

Contents

Foreword

Lee will always have a warm and special place in our memory at Sierra Veterinary Hospital. He was a stabilizing influence at Animal Control during Carson City's growth and change from rural to urban lifestyle. Such things as enforcing leash laws, negotiating the neighborhood disputes, providing education for pet protection, and saving 'hurt critters' were all in a day's work for Lee Wittek. We will miss you Lee!

Woodrow ("Woody") J. Allen, D.V.M.

Lee was a fine gentleman, ready to be your best friend or lock horns to the end, depending on you. The true size of his heart comes through in this short rendition of his life.

Gary L. Ailes, D.V.M.

I had the privilege of knowing Lee Wittek for the last fifteen years of his life. He was a friend and an individual with an uncommon devotion to the care and well-being of animals. One could not help but absorb some of Lee's compassion just by being around him. In fact, over the years I acquired two wonderful stray dogs that Lee brought to me, injured and in need of veterinary care, and that were never claimed. All of us in Carson City, animal and human, are better off having had Lee as an Animal Control officer. I know he helped me raise the 'iron curtain' many times, and I hope I did the same for him.

John H. Margolin, D.V.M.

Acknowledgments

I T IS TRUE that no man is an island unto himself. And so it is that with a deep appreciation of the value of friends, I am able to acknowledge the contributions of others to the completion of this work.

But first, I give to Glenna, my beloved wife, my heartfelt thanks for being the burr under my saddle which constantly moved me forward.

Appreciation tenfold also goes to Syd Brown for the photos and graphics, as well as design and typography in this volume.

And finally, thanks also to Maggie Mitchell, who is the hidden dynamo that powered the engine that produced this work, truly a joint venture.

Introduction

WHAT DO animal Control Officers really do? Lee Wittek answers that via *Critter Capers*, a chronicle of his many adventures and misadventures during two decades of rescuing dogs, cats, horses and other, mostly small, creatures. Given his druthers, Wittek would have adopted them all.

Friends remember Wittek for his sly humor and deep compassion for animals, both of which spill over into this collection of the many tales he recorded during his duties in Carson City (Nevada), giving warm insight into the rarely publicized Animal Control profession. It is a heartwarming tribute to dogcatchers everywhere.

"I'm tired of walking. I know where the
dog-catcher lives. He'll give us a ride home."

TIPS FROM THE DOGCATCHER'S WIFE

"You haven't lived," Glenna claims, "until you wake up one morning to find yourself married to an Animal Control Officer—to discover that strange noise outside is a horse tethered to your cosmopolitan front door, or to realize that you've just been anointed masseuse-of-choice to administer an emergency de-scenting tomato juice bath to your hapless spouse because he failed to zig when a startled skunk zagged. In the process, you'll also need a sponge-off with that same traditional antidote. It may not be spa-chic but it's guaranteed to restore you to perfumery level!"

"ADMITTEDLY, SHE'S RIGHT," agrees Lee. Animal Control has its fallout on wives. It isn't just another day at the office. In fact, no two days are alike, each conjuring its own unique rescues, problems and solutions.

For instance, there's the shrill off-duty beeper that invariably shatters tranquility at inconvenient moments. Add the nagging concern for the welfare of a rescued injured pet, hoping against hope that it survives.

Leading with your heart on animal control is a no-no. I call it 'pulling down the iron curtain.' Rescue, lend assistance, but don't get emotionally involved. Ignore the pleading eyes that beg to be taken home, to share their unconditional devotion. But to an animal lover, that's a tall order. It's iron-curtain time half a dozen times a day. Do veterinarians have the same problem?

So prudence dictates an efficient, detached professional approach to frightened, injured creatures. And don't adopt them all. There isn't enough room at home for them. Wives tend to object. They're funny that way.

But thank you, Glenna, for your infinite patience through it all. I love you......

Lee

"A Perfect World means owning a warm lap."

THE INITIATION

Where is the beginning? For me, it was at the end of too many years spent chasing dollars in the fields of commerce. An item in the paper provided the inspiration. Animal Control had an opening. I liked animals, be they stray mutts or Frank Buck prey. Why not? I took the leap. And, variety being the spice of life, I hit the jackpot.

FOR STARTERS there was The Filcher, the cayenne of variety. I cannot even remember what kind of dog he was, but as I recall, he was just a vision of medium-size brown.

It all happened on Magnolia Way, a street lined with aging apartment houses with here and there a private dwelling. The structures were old style, that is, they were buildings without grounds or patio areas. So, if you wanted to do something out-doors, such as barbecue, you just opened your door, stepped outside and did it, practically on the sidewalk.

This particular unit had a back door so you could merely venture outside and barbecue in the parking lot. That's what this gentleman was trying to do early one summer evening. Just a little home-grilled steak, that's all he wanted.

Well, the old Filcher had the same idea. However, being a dog had its drawbacks as he just did not have the ability to grill his own supper. No matter. Here was a human doing it for him. He's really some kind of nice guy, Filcher thought, and whisked the steak right off the grill while Mr. Nice Guy was inside drawing another beer and didn't even see the brown blur that took off with his fillet.

Imagine his surprise, to say nothing of chagrin, when he came back outside to check the results of his culinary efforts.

Undaunted, he put another steak on the grill, resolving to keep a closer eye on it. But, ever observant, Filcher did it again only this time right under the watchful eye of Mr. Nice Guy who was now not so nice.

A frenzied chase was on but at its conclusion the Nice Guy had nothing to show for his efforts but an empty grill and a lot of huffing and puffing. So Animal Control was called and I responded.

The capture was easy since The Filcher was hanging around again, being not only friendly but somewhat piggish, hoping futilely for another handout.

I was just closing the rear door to the Animal Control van when a couple of ruffians clutched me from behind and tossed me a good eight feet backward. To say that I was stunned is to put it mildly.

I sat on my keister in the middle of the parking lot and, momentarily befuddled, watched some burly character rescue The Filcher from my truck as both sluggers then took off for the hills. By the time I collected my wits and followed in pursuit, it was too late. The scoundrels had disappeared.

It was my first week on the job and you can bet your paycheck that I had some serious second thoughts about this spicy new Animal Control career on which I was embarking!

THAT WAS IN SHARP CONTRAST TO DASH, one of my favorites in the variety memory bank. I met him through Charlie, a rancher with a large spread on the outskirts of town. Charlie just happened to live close to the intersection of two highways, a junction that seemed to be a magnet for anybody who wanted to dump a dog, figuring it would be taken care of.

And Charlie usually did, temporarily at least. That's when our paths would frequently cross, unofficially, because he lived out of my jurisdiction. But, having known him for many years, he would give me one of his periodic calls anyway.

"Somebody dumped another dog," he'd begin. "Right pretty one too. But I can't keep it. D'ya know anybody who would?"

And, luck being with me, I frequently did, somebody who probably couldn't afford an impound fee but would give the animal a good home. But in this latest instance, Charlie was more hesitant.

"I'd really like to keep this one," he went on, "but I've already got three good ones. It's a Collie, damned nice dog too. I named him Dash."

On my day off I paid a visit to Dash. And I had to agree, he was a fine specimen of dogdom.

"I'll look around," I promised Charlie, without having the slightest idea who would want a duplicate version of Lassie.

A couple of days later a chance conversation with Bernie, a newcomer, caught my attention.

"How's the new operation going?" I inquired, knowing he had just purchased a small ranch.

"Great," he said, "but now I need another dog. One that can maybe work cattle." I thought of Dash.

"I can't promise," I warned, "but Charlie, down at the intersection, has a stray Collie he's willing to part with. He says it a pretty good dog."

That's all the information Bernie needed. The next time I encountered him in town he was all raves.

"Hey, that Dash worked out great!" he greeted me. "He promptly fell in love with my border dog, Matilda, and they work the pasture together. Where one is, you'll always find the other one!"

It was weeks later before I ran across him again. This time he came into the Shelter. He seemed downcast.

"What's the problem?" I inquired.

"Remember Dash?" he began. I nodded. "One day he came up to the house barkin'. That was unusual for him. So when he kept it up, I followed him down to the pasture. There was Matilda. She had probably been killed by coyotes. Dash just laid down beside her and wouldn't move."

I expressed my condolences as I sensed Bernie was quite upset. "So I guess you'll be looking for another dog?" I ventured.

"Two of them," he said gloomily.

"Two?" I asked in surprise.

"Yeah," he answered, half-heartedly, and told me the rest of the tale.

Dash, it seemed, was so totally devoted to Matilda he wouldn't leave her side, even in death, even to come up to the house to eat. So Bernie carried food and water down to him. But Dash wouldn't touch a bite. He just stood watch by Matilda's still form and even objected when Bernie went down to give her a proper burial under the big cottonwood tree where they frequently hung out.

Once buried, Dash took his position on Matilda's grave and again, refused to budge. Bernie was at wit's end trying to accommodate the faithful Collie but nothing he did would move Dash from his watch.

Several more days of carrying food and water down to the pasture brought about an unexpected end to the episode. On the fourth day Bernie found Dash, his lifeless form encompassing Matilda's grave. There were no marks on his body. No coyotes had devastated him. Dash, apparently, had just died of a broken heart. That's when Bernie buried him, next to Matilda, along with a few of his own tears.

THEN THERE WAS DEPUTY, another one of those creatures that remain unexplainably memorable. Magnificent in stature, he was one of the few dogs to cross my path that refused to be pampered or cajoled into friendship. That old shep did things his way, and never lost his mean streak, to my knowledge.

He originally belonged to the caretaker at Animal Control, and he was a darned good watchdog. One glimpse of that big German Shepherd gliding soundlessly across the compound toward the gate was enough to cause any prowler to go prowl elsewhere.

Deputy never growled, never barked. He just kept on coming—silent, alert, watchful. You knew he meant business. And he certainly did.

We locked horns early on. But after he bit me for the third time in as many days, we decided that he just couldn't hang around the Shelter any longer.

He really didn't bite hard. It was more like a nonfriendly pressure of jaws around the wrist that promised more if you didn't pay attention and leave. Quickly.

Still, he had to go and it looked pretty grim for old Dep because a dog of his temperament would be difficult if not impossible to place for adoption. It was 'iron-curtain' time for sure as Dep was definitely on his way out, one way or another.

Then he got lucky. We found a rare jewel in a new master, one who was tougher than Deputy and who had a place where a dog of Dep's capability was needed.

On trial run, the two worked beautifully together. Deputy minded his manners when his master was around and let everyone else know they weren't welcome when left on his own.

It was the kind of culmination we like to see since the life of every animal is precious.

"Now wag fast. The air conditioning is broken."

THE STOVEPIPE DID IT

It's lunch time, not mine, but everybody else's. I'm manning the desk. We don't close the kennel during lunch hour as it might irritate the public, especially if a pet dog or cat has been impounded and its owner uses a lunch hour to come in and retrieve it. It wouldn't be kosher to find the shelter door adorned with an 'OUT TO LUNCH' sign. So, we stagger our hours in order to be available for the entire day. It is good public policy with the added benefit that we might adopt out a dog or cat that perhaps would not otherwise be placed.

SOON EVERYBODY WAS BACK from lunch but before I could get out of the office, the phone rang. It was a code response. That means it gets answered now. And now means NOW! On this particular day I was the only field officer on duty so forget about lunch.

Such cases usually concern an injured animal but other emergencies do arise that require immediate action. This was one of those, even though the request indicated no animal injury. The reporting party said that a dog had jammed its head into a pipe of some sort and was stuck and that it was beginning to howl loud enough to upset the whole neighborhood. Could we send someone right away? We could. We did. I was it.

I was directed to a strip of land bordering the local airport runway, a segment which separates the airport from a residential area. It was about a half mile wide and constituted a buffer zone for air traffic safety. It was typically desert, full of sagebrush, field mice and other miscellany.

Some folks also thought such a tract was a good place to dump their trash without having to pay a fee at the landfill. One of the items there that day happened to be an old wall furnace.

The dog in question, it seems, thought this would be a good place to spend an afternoon chasing critters, sniffing burrows and other doggy diversions. After all, it had taken a lot of work digging that hole under his own back yard fence and he wasn't about to waste all that effort just hanging around home. So off to the airport field he went.

Sure enough, predictably, he spotted a young jackrabbit and the chase was on.

A word to those who are unfamiliar with rabbits. Be advised they are fast. They also cheat. They refuse to run in a straight line and give an ambitious dog a sporting chance to use his superior long-range speed. Instead, rabbits shift, dodge and go through small holes in the sagebrush that no self-respecting dog would even attempt. To add insult to injury, rabbits will sometimes just stop altogether and sit down as soon as they break out of the dog's line of vision, which of course, leaves the poor dog running in a straight line 500 feet ahead of the rabbit. Thus, it takes a really good dog to run down a rabbit.

The dog in question was a good dog. Or maybe the pursued bunny was one of the slower ones. At any rate, the dog was rapidly gaining footage when it became apparent to the rabbit that his end was near, pardon the pun.

Desperate measures were clearly called for. That's when the long-eared lagomorph spotted this dark hole in an object lying in his path and without regard for consequences, zip, in he went for sanctuary. Undaunted, although not with a great show of wisdom, said dog went in after him. Well, almost in—instead burying himself up to his shoulders.

What he had jammed himself into was the heating chamber of a discarded wall furnace. It was the old-fashioned kind once used in motel rooms, the kind with louvered panels at top and bottom. There was also a horizontal hole in the exhaust pipe with a collar fitted onto it. Entering it was not as simple as merely running into the opening. It was more like running into a hole in the side of it, with the added distinction of a tricky exit.

Compare it to those Chinese novelties that look like a tube of woven straw, the kind where you stick one finger in from either end but when you try to pull the finger out, the tube tightens and the finger is trapped. The harder you pull, the more the tube constricts.

So the poor dog had sort of gotten himself into just such a Chinese tube. His head had barely squeezed into that hole in the side. Once inside, there was plenty of room, but backing out was another matter as his ears and bunched-up skin around the head made more volume going out than going in, no doubt a canine humiliator. The rabbit sat at the opposite end of the pipe, smirking and twitching its little button nose.

That's what I found when I arrived on the scene. I tried gently pulling on the dog but that was no go. I tried working out the folds in its hide, hoping to reduce his size where he was stuck in the pipe, but no luck.

Emergency measures were clearly needed. That's when I went to a nearby residence and borrowed a bottle of liquid soap. This method usually works. Just lather up the dog's neck good and bubbly, and coat the edge of the hole as well. Now pull and pop! Out comes the dog! But not this time. The diameter of the hole was too small and the diameter of the dog too large. I tried working out the dog a fold of skin at a time but for every inch of progress, the dog would lurch toward the rabbit and ruin it. The rabbit just smirked some more.

It soon became obvious the dog would have to be cut out so I returned to my van and radioed the Fire department to assist. They arrived with enough equipment to clear a freeway pile-up, but the only thing I needed was a good pair of tin snips, which they had.

The idea was to cut the tin, taking care to avoid snipping the wiggling dog. It works great in theory. In practice, the operation agitates and frightens the dog. The result can be a panicky animal that may bite savagely once its head is cleared of the retainer. Caution is therefore the order of the moment.

Rather than try to cut a larger circle in the pipe, I cut chunks out of the collar around the hole. I figured that if the metal were weakened sufficiently, the pulling action would bend it and allow the dog to slip out. So I gave that a try but there was still too much metal tension. Then another cut here, a snip there, and it was time to try again.

One of the firemen got a good grip on the dog's hindquarters and I got a firm one on his neck just above the shoulders and together we gently pulled and wiggled. Slowly, the metal gave way and the dog's head started to emerge. It was like a birthing only there was no umbilical cord to cut.

Suddenly it was over. Mr. Dog was free. We left the rabbit to work his own way out, which he did in a hurry as soon as we backed off enough for him to feel safe. The dog was so glad to be rescued he didn't even notice his quarry's departure, but you can bet the hare had quite a tale to tell his family when he got home that night!

"Now don't start nagging, Queenie.
I've had a bad hare day..."

TREED

Disney said it best. It's a small, small world.

 **SHE WALKED OUT** into the early sunlight to fetch the morning paper. One good thing about that publication's carriers: They always get your paper in the general proximity of your neighborhood.

She knew she should have put on her glasses first, but so what? She only needed them to see with. And the morning paper in its colorful plastic wrapper was a different hue than the driveway or the lawn. So, she figured she should be able to spot it.

And spot it she did. She also saw the neighbor's cat in her tree. It was the tree far down on the corner of the adjoining lot where the two driveways converged.

Her first thought was that the cat had certainly grown bigger. Taking another look, she concluded that perhaps it was her neighbor's yellow Lab. But what was it doing in a tree?

Her next and obviously correct observation was that she was doing a lousy job of observing without her glasses so then and there she decided to resolve the dilemma. She went into the house, fetched the spectacles and came back outside. That's when she turned in mid-stride and dashed back into the house for some 9-1-1 time. What she saw was not a cat or a yellow Lab. What that yellow thing was, when she was able to see properly, was a mountain lion!

There are a number of reasons, I suppose, why a mountain lion might be in your tree in the middle of town but it's rather academic to argue about them. It's just there and that's usually not a fitting state of affairs.

I was off duty so the the dispatcher called me at home and I called Nevada Fish and Game Department before I left the house. Mountain lions, or cougars, are not, I repeat, not within the jurisdiction of Animal Control. We do dogs and house cats. We wear badges. We enforce laws that are written for us to read so we know what to enforce. Cougars, natch, do not respect badges and don't give a hoot about uniforms or written-down laws. That's why we generally do not answer wildlife calls.

But, we do have a duty to protect the public health and safety and, while it is questionable that our little aluminum poles with loops on them are adequate tools with which to handle big bad cats, there is a small justification for our being there. We are acknowledged specialists in the field of animal handling. So much for status!

Anyway, I arrived on the scene first and took up a position at the base of the tree to stare at the cat. There is a strange thing about these big creatures, or so the lore says. When a cat, big or small, is treed, that is, up a tree, it really likes to stay there, like glue. It reputedly does not want to escape from the relative safety of such a perch since it fails to equate just being up a tree as equivalent to being cornered.

All I could do was stand and stare and wait for more help. I did have a bit of assistance from one of the ever-increasing number of neighbors who were congregating in the yard. It was an offer to get a ladder. Luckily, it was a twelve-footer.

Pretty soon the warden from Fish and Game arrived and we conferred on strategy. It was decided that the warden would shoot the cat with a nonlethal dose of tranquilizer and that thereafter we would climb the tree and remove the drowsy cat. The warden, being a big guy who would weigh down the small branches and I, being the smaller guy, guess who got to go first and highest?

Actually, the capture turned out to be quite easy. Once the big cat was drowsy, I went up the first twelve feet on the ladder and the last few in the tree itself. I looped the cat and dragged his limp body out of the fork where he had perched. He was so far gone that he could be cradled in arms like a baby. As a matter of fact, he was only a young'un and didn't weigh much over 50 pounds. We soon had him in the truck and on his way to a relocation area, tied up, of course.

As for the Disney angle, just about ten days after this episode my son decided he needed a haircut. So he went to his usual barber emporium which was one of the older style shops where conversation goes along with the trim job. Barbers are like bartenders. They have something in common with Father Confessors and psychologists. Everybody wants to talk to them.

So the barber queried one customer about his trip and if he saw anything interesting en route. That's when a guy in an adjacent chair interrupted and related an anecdote about how on *his* trip in a place called Carson City, which is the capital of the State of Nevada where they're supposed to be civilized, a mountain lion was found in the middle of town and was dragged out of a tree by a dogcatcher. How quaint can they get out there in the High Desert?

Is it truly a small world? The barber shop was in Orlando, Florida! My son, knowing of the incident, just sat there quietly beaming, "That's my Pop!"

LYNCH HIM!

*It happened on a lane called Sigma which is
named after one of the earliest working ranches
in the area. For all I know, the road might once
have been just a country lane on the ranch. In any
case, it exists today and goes just a short distance
from there to here. It connects two busy arteries
and enjoys a bit of traffic itself because of it.*

EARLY ONE MORNING we received a call from an indignant lady
who was, to put it politely, fit to be tied. She had seen something
on Sigma Lane that struck her as the worst case of animal
abuse she had ever heard of, let alone actually witnessed with her
own eyes.

She had been traveling on said Lane, going from there to
here on her way to work, and off to one side of the road she
espied a large red barn with its doors wide open. The open doors
caught her attention, for in the past she had often noticed the red
structure without particular interest. It was so commonplace as to
be unremarkable, that is, until today. The open doors drew her
attention and she was both shocked and sickened by what she
saw within. Some cruelly sadistic person had hung his horse!

Surely, this expletive-deleted person had to be punished for
the dastardly deed, preferably by hanging. At least that was this
lady's opinion, one which was shared off-hand by members of our
staff as well. It sounded like a deserving idea to me too. After all,
there are more humane ways to put down an ailing equine.

As it turned out, it was to be my assignment to track down
the culprit and, while I did not disagree with the commonly held
opinion that the miscreant be hanged, I was just a mite nervous
about it since I was a neophyte in the enforcement business at the
time and I had not, as yet, hung anybody.

I did not want to blow my case by using improper procedures nor did I feel too comfortable just barging into that barn, so I guessed I'd just have to play it by ear when I got there.

The place wasn't too hard to find since the lane is a short one and there were only two barn-like structures on the whole stretch and only one of them was red. I had hoped the doors to the barn would be open and I could catch the guy red-handed, so to speak. But luck was not with me. The barn doors were too tightly closed. No help there, so up to the house I went.

The gentleman who answered the door was just a bit older than I and while he was polite, he obviously was uncertain as to the reason an Animal Control Officer would be standing on his doorstep.

I advised him that he had a right not to talk to me under the Miranda decision and I offered to read him his Miranda rights but he surprised me saying, "What the heck. Ask anything you want."

His 'I've got nothing to hide' attitude rang rather hollow since I knew what he had hanging in his barn.

It seemed to me that he was making my job pretty easy by his too-willing cooperation and so when I asked permission to check his barn, his ready agreement perplexed me. And, sure enough, when he swung the big red doors wide open, there hung a horse, suspended from a big wooden beam by two wide leather straps looped under the belly. The horse was dead.

It was just as dead as Roy Rogers' Trigger and for just about the same period of time as well. Like Roy, this guy had loved his horse and when it died, he had it mounted by a taxidermist. To him, the horse was symbolic of his youth and his lingering love for the animal.

But why hang it? Because at ground level the mice were nibbling at its feet and to protect it, he suspended it from the rafters. Case closed!

I wonder, did Roy encounter the same turmoil from his neighbors when he preserved Trigger for posterity?

THE MEANEST MAN

*To die alone is obviously sad. But to die alone
and have no one who cares is a tragedy.*

WALTER IS DEAD, arguably the meanest man in town, the local
version of Scrooge. I knew of no one who would mourn his passing. And that, in itself, is the saddest commentary that can be
made about his life and the emptiness of it.

Walter was large of girth and small in spirit, the milk of
human kindness appearing never to have touched his lips. Whatever charity and tolerance that may once have been his forte had
long since dried up, withered.

It is probably true that he brought it all on himself for he
was mean. He *was* petty. He was also selfish in the smallest sense
of the word. He never missed an opportunity to spitefully use or
abuse his fellow man.

It would have taken a battery of psychiatrists to dig out the
root causes of the anger and frustration which he vented so freely
on those around him. It was there with him always. He wore it
seemingly as a badge of honor, like a suit of clothing for everyone
to see and he cared not a whit that they saw it. It is no small
wonder that no one will miss him.

When the lady who lived across the street took in a couple of
kids for day care to supplement the family income, Walter
promptly called both the children's services and the business
licensing offices to put a stop to it.

The Health Department was on a first name basis with
Walter who routinely phoned whenever any neighbor dared let the

grass grow too tall or allow a pile of autumn leaves to accumulate for too long.

He even parked his pickup truck sideways in his driveway close to the sidewalk, no easy feat in itself, to prohibit little tykes from using his drive to turn around their trikes and Big Wheels.

Nothing escaped his attention or his belligerence. He stood guard behind drawn curtains, constantly alert for any transgressions upon his sacred rights.

Unfortunately, one of my most embarrassing incidents involved him, at least in a minor way. It just made the whole matter much worse to have had Walter involved.

To start with, I had allowed the unforgivable to happen. As we used to say in the military, "No excuse, Sir!" My dog, Soupy, was in heat. It should never have been allowed, and most assuredly, not by me of all people. But it happened.

Soupy was the ultimate escape artist, a regular Houdini at getting out of the house, even though I had been taking extra precautions to see to it that she didn't even get a chance to contemplate it.

But I grossly underestimated her cleverness. She was a jet black curly-coated dog that we call a bend-over because you had to bend down to pet her. It was nearly impossible to see her in the dark except by looking for her eyes or listening for the sound of her thumping tail, which was all matted down and looked like a rat's appendage instead of a dog's. That's because she knocked the hair flat with her constant joyous thumping. No amount of brushing or combing could make it look like a canine tail.

As Fate would have it, one early twilight evening Soupy got out. Being not quite dark yet but only dim, Soupy was about to do the invisible act. My daughter had left a few moments earlier and Soupy divined, correctly as it turned out, that I would soon follow, so she stationed herself near the front door. No thumping of tail, no panting, head down so I couldn't see her eyes, just waiting ever so quietly.

Apparently, as I slipped carefully out the door, so did Soup. She obviously just sat down again and waited, not moving an inch, until I got far enough away not to notice that she had escaped.

Shortly thereafter while on an errand, I spotted Soupy. Heaven forbid, she had chosen to meet her boyfriend in Walter's front yard and was still there in happy rendezvous when I spied her. The shameless hussy could not have picked a worse place for her romance. I bolted from the car and across the yard just in time to nearly collide with good old Walter as he charged furiously out of his front door to put a stop to this outrage which was being committed on his very own turf.

Walter aimed a vicious kick at the two dogs and I barely got a shoulder into his in time to divert the blow. We had a few choice words for each other but this was a time for action, not words.

And the action didn't really belong against Walter. After all, Soupy's escape was my fault, doubly so. But to escape Walter's wrath, I scooped up both dogs, united as they were, threw them bodily into the car through the open window and sped away with Walter shaking his fist after my fleeing form.

So now, what to do with two amorous dogs in the back seat? I guess I was rattled and not thinking too straight. I couldn't very well take Soupy home and try to break up this romance there.

I just drove to the nearest carwash and, looking completely foolish I'm sure, stuck the station's water hose into the back seat and let fly. Needless to say, I attracted some curious glances but by that time I was beyond caring.

Finally, the dogs broke up their liaison, cooled down after nearly drowning, and I beat a hasty retreat from the station. I was getting pretty good at retreating. Figuring that Soupy's boyfriend must live in the area where they had met, I returned there and put the hapless, sopping wet dog out on the sidewalk. Then I headed for home with Soupy.

It didn't work. Sitting on my front step, waiting for me to bring his girlfriend back was one sexually unsatisfied, thoroughly wet dog.

This was too much to be borne and I took off with a drenched companion in the back seat and another one in hot pursuit. I hit speeds of up to 30 miles an hour along the residential streets with no luck. That dog could literally fly.

A good mile later I still had not lost him. He could not only run, he could endure. He charged gamely along behind the car, tail straight out in the breeze, tongue dripping and chest heaving but still coming on.

I stopped and took him in. What else was a fella to do? He sat, patiently waiting, in my front yard most of the night, then finally gave up and was gone by morning.

But Walter was not gone. Precisely at the Shelter's opening time the next morning, he showed up in person to complain about the atrocity which had occurred on his very own property the night before. An outrage!

For some strange reason, perhaps because he had always seen me in uniform, he had not recognized me in street clothes the previous evening and did not know that I was the same person who had confronted him in his own yard. I was far too embarrassed to correct that oversight and so listened sympathetically to his tale of woe.

That was my last encounter with Walter for quite some time. Meanwhile, Soupy had a little visit to the vet's so that problem would never again arise.

When the news spread regarding Walter's eventual demise, nobody cared, including me.

But wait. It seems that I was wrong. There is one who mourned. There was one solitary figure that stood by him in life and in death as well, one who sat and kept silent vigil over the still, lifeless body of his master, his friend. He alone was there waiting, unwilling to accept the fact that the soul inside was gone and that only mortal flesh remained.

Indeed, the meanest man in town had a companion, a dog, his own best friend. Is there anywhere upon the globe a more loyal compatriot than a dog? Is there anywhere a friend who will love you more, cherish you more, even though you may deserve it less? Who else would give so much to receive so little if it not be your dog? Do you know of a human who would do that much just for the love of you?

For three days and for all of those three long nights, the dog had sat poised beside his master's still form, waiting in vain for Walter to awaken. Reluctantly, he finally allowed himself to be coaxed away. Warily, he gave up his master.

May God bless the dog and bless the man who can call one his friend. Maybe the meanest man in town wasn't so mean after all.

"Just because you're a snapping turtle
doesn't mean you have to be
cranky all the time!"

STRANGE COMPANIONS

SNOOPER headed the list of the least likely critters to be adopted as a pet. He arrived as an adjunct to an Easter basket. Of course, he was a bunny, sporting soft white fur that just invited petting.

And he became a very loving and friendly pet, living in the house as a bona fide member of the family. His playmate was the family dog, a Great Dane-Doberman mix, a most unlikely cohort.

Rabbits incidentally, are very clean as house pets as they adapt to a litter pan as readily as cats.

Snooper especially liked to have his silky coat groomed. Just say, "Let's comb your hair" and Snoop would come hopping over and jump up into the nearest lap. He loved to be held and stroked and believed that anyone sitting down was fair game for that diversion, regularly scrambling up onto any handy knee and pestering until he was thus accommodated.

Snooper was also a practical joker. He liked to sneak up and untie the shoe laces of any unsuspecting victim. His favorite food was Italian parsley and his favorite treats were mineral stones.

"Snooper was warm and loving," says his former owner. "He brought much happiness to anyone fortunate enough to be around him. Never was a bunny so loved and pampered as much as Snooper. We miss him more than words can say and just hope the angels take good care of him. He was a light that shone too briefly."

AND WHILE RUSTY didn't start out life as a pet, he took to it readily. It all started one day when Brownie, the family dog who was still mourning the giveaway of her litter of pups, came home carrying this wiggly little bundle of cinnamon fur.

"When she proudly deposited it at our feet," said the dog's owner, "we were astonished to see it was a tiny wild rabbit."

But what to do with it? It was too small to get around by itself. But Brownie soon took care of that. She just carried it over to a corner of the porch and deposited the wee one in the box formerly occupied by her pups and proceeded to nurse and otherwise pamper it until we supplied rabbit pellets. Dubbed 'Rusty,' it soon won the hearts of the whole family.

But its mere presence in such outdoor quarters caused a dilemma of sorts since a neighbor's free-roaming hound dog was a rabbit freak and as a result, frequently clashed with Brownie who became overly protective of her unique charge. But sometimes Nature has a way of solving such problems.

Rusty grew rapidly and more and more, began to roam the outer reaches, first of the lawn, then the orchard, always accompanied by Brownie. Then one day Brownie was spotted alongside Rusty at the fringes of the little creek. The bunny took a few more hops, then turned to Brownie, as though inviting the dog to come along. Brownie hesitated, watching her chum.

But the call of the wild was too strong. Rusty hopped a few more lengths, then turned and issued one last cordial invitation. Brownie hesitated again, momentarily debating her next move. Then she sat down, resolutely. She would stay put and finally seemed willing to let her offbeat little companion go his way. Rusty gave vent to a few more hops, turned for one last good-bye to Brownie, then was gone.

"We never saw Rusty again," his former benefactors stated, "and hope he had a long and happy life."

THE OUTCASTS

THERE'S A FIRST TIME for everything.

The huge drill bit went 'round and 'round, chewing its way ever deeper into the earth. The resulting hole, when finished, would receive a couple hundred pounds or so of wet concrete and a very tall lamp post which would serve as one half of the ornate gateway to the new, and prestigious housing development.

'Prestigious' is a fancy word meaning expensive. In this case, add 'very' in front of 'expensive.' To live in this neighborhood would require a lot of zeroes in annual income and they would mostly have to be to the left of the decimal point. Unless, of course, you happened to live down below.

Down below was being exceedingly disturbed as the huge drill bit disrupted the underground home of one of the original residents of the area. She had been there long before the developers arrived and she was most dismayed at this recent turn of events.

She watched helplessly as all of the living room and most of the two adjoining bedrooms were chewed up and spit out by the churning bit.

Soon it was all over. The home, or at least a major portion of it, was gone and the departing drill left behind nothing but a little dust and a huge hole. Admonishing her children to stay away from the hole beneath where the living room had been, Momma went to the front door to assess whatever damage might have occurred there and to see if new danger lurked outside.

Then the obvious surfaced: Never trust a kid. Especially, never trust three of them working together to get, quite deliberately, into mischief. First one, then two, then three in a row tumbled into the hole. Imagine Mom's dismay when she returned to find all her little ones down inside the deep excavation.

It was like three kids in a well. But Momma was the heroine. She jumped into the hole to rescue her family only to find that she was in just as much trouble as they were. None of them could climb up and out. In desperation she began to holler for help, a series of desperate wails, until someone noticed her plight.

When that happened, our office was called and I inherited the assignment. As soon as I arrived on the scene and assessed the situation I knew that this was one of those rescues of which my wife was so fond—the inevitable tomato juice bath! At least it had all the potential.

The rotating drill had cleared a hole about two feet below what used to be the living room, which was originally about three feet or more down. This was a job for the capture pole and I would have to be positioned directly over the top of the well-like opening, maybe even part way inside. Momma skunk and her three little ones waited expectantly. My only questions were: Would she shoot? And how straight?

Perhaps, contrary to convention, she understood that this was help, not hindrance, for she allowed me to put the loop around her and lift her ever so gently out of the hole. As soon as she was elevated to ground level, I covered her with a blanket, just in case, and off-loaded her into a nearby carrier which stood open and ready.

For some strange reason, not one of the many curious people standing around offered to assist. Soon all three kids were also safely inside the carrier with Mom and we were all off to the woods for a habitat release. For the record, it was my first skunk encounter in which I returned home in the same pristine uniform in which I left.

THERE IS ANOTHER CRITTER that is accused of shooting people. It's the porcupine. Many a dog has found, to its dismay, that porcupines are not for play. A mouthful of quills is just about the most painful state imaginable for dogs that have fallen victim to a porcupine. Fortunately for most canines, it is a short-lived experience. A trip to the vet, a good knockout shot and a pair of pliers soon repair the damage, at least to the mouth if not to the dog's self-esteem.

The most useful tool ever invented for an Animal Control Officer is known as the 'Come-a-Long,' a pole with a pulley loop enabling a rescuer to simply stand a few feet away and place the loop carefully over the animal so that it can then be guided safely to the van.

When doing this to a porcupine, it expands its body which causes all the quills to stand on end like a cartoon character's hair. This little routine makes it difficult to get the loop around the stubborn rodent and also makes an officer tend to be very certain the loop is correctly placed before moving the animal.

In spite of great care, it is axiomatic that an officer will likely find himself victim of a quill or two. They are not exactly barbed on the sharp end but they are rough and are difficult to remove. That is why pliers are used for that chore.

The injury-free trick in removing a porcupine from an unwanted locale is to set a box trap and transport the offender, still in the box, to a new location. Open the box, stand back, and just let it go out on its own.

But contrary to popular myth, porcupines do not shoot their quills. The quills are shed rather easily. A mere touch will do it. And the animal will slap at you with its tail, which is where the quills are the loosest. But they do not shoot them, not even if they see the whites of your eyes!

"The new cat door seems to work
just fine..."

IN THE CULVERT

Heavy wet clouds hung low over the Sierra. A large cold air mass gradually drew them down the eastern slopes, a portent that the valley below was going to get wet. It was this impending storm that made the anxious Shepherd's position perilous.

IT SEEMS THAT Momma Shep was a stray and, fearful of human interference, had decided that the culvert would provide a sanctuary for her newly born brood. She was partly right, for her abode was nearly unapproachable by anything big enough to endanger her. Unfortunately, she had not allowed for the vagaries of Mother Nature who had ideas of her own and was about to dump a few tons of water into the wash leading to the culvert. The stage was set for disaster.

When Mack and I arrived, we found Momma smack dab in the middle of a 60-foot long corrugated metal pipe running under the driveway leading to a motorhome park. Mack took one quick look at the setting and, hands on hips, announced "It's all yours, Lee!"

Being not too obtuse, I could see the logic of his pronouncement. Mack has the chest and shoulders of an iron pusher and could not have, from any angle, forced that much mass into that small pipe. It would have been tantamount to putting toothpaste back into the tube.

I, on the other hand, being somewhat of smaller stature, could even fit into one of those suits of armor found in museums so I knew I could squirm into the culvert.

Armed with a shovel to use as a prod, I commenced the crawl to the middle of the pipe where Momma and the kids were hiding. The plan was simple. Prod Momma with the shovel and she goes out the other end of the pipe, whereupon the kids can be rescued. Shows you how wrong a guy can be.

It was a tight fit, even for me, as sand from previous flooding had layered the bottom of the pipe and further reduced its meager dimensions. I could barely manage to crawl caterpillar style, using my elbows and feet as propellers.

Meanwhile, Momma Shepherd just sat quietly in the middle of the gloomy culvert, watching my slow approach. It was too dark to count heads but a number of pups were busy doing what pups do.

Finally I reached the point where I could begin to persuade Momma to exit so I gently extended the shovel toward her. That's when all hell broke loose and this gentle mother dog turned instantly into a frenzied bundle of teeth. Anyone conversant with physics knows that tooth enamel clashing on steel will not create sparks. If it could have, Cave Man would have chewed fire into existence instead of discovering flint. But I'll forever swear that sparks flew inside that dim hollow pipe. Momma's head grew huge and seemed to fill the pipe entirely as she tried to get past the blade of my feebly jabbing shovel to drive me out. My movements were restricted by the narrow confines of the culvert and I feared for my safety if she got past the shovel. Feared? I was scared stiff, the kind of fright that puts feet into action to go anywhere but where I was.

But there was nowhere to go except back and I couldn't go back without using my hands and elbows in that reverse caterpillar crawl which would mean losing control over the shovel. If she got past the point of the shovel, there was nothing with which to fend off her threatening attack except my hands and face. In an emergency, I could smack her with my nose. That would take care of her slashing teeth. Great strategy! Again, again and again: three times in all, she hunched her body and lunged toward me before she gave up. Finally I could start to retreat in relative safety.

Outside, safe and standing in the soft rain that had now begun, I knew that I would not go back in there. Mack's advice was to forget it. He said that the rain would fill the wash slowly and force her out. I suspected he didn't believe it but he said it anyway. He knew that I was lucky not to have been seriously chewed up. But we were both reluctant to give up. We felt that Mom would likely get out OK, but would she be able to rescue the pups?

Mack suggested that we get something long to push into the pipe and suddenly the answer was born whole in my mind. Up to the park's office we went to talk to its manager. We needed some stuff that he almost certainly had on hand, judging by the landscaping that surrounded the park. Could we borrow the needed items? We soon found out that he did indeed have the stuff and that we could make use of it. He too, had been concerned about the pups, which had triggered his call to us initially.

Back at the culvert's mouth I placed an empty five-gallon plastic bucket into the mouth of the pipe, with the closed end facing the dogs. Next Mack and I pushed it in, using PVC pipe in 20-foot lengths. Another pipe, another 20 feet. Mack moved over to the other end where Momma would come out, we hoped, and got ready to loop her if and when she did. We believed that the bucket would slide over the pups but would squeeze Momma out, that is, unless the bucket slid over her as well. Remember the toothpaste analogy? Here it was again, only in reverse. The bucket pushed Momma out the end of the culvert just like toothpaste coming out of a tube. Mack looped her and put her into the van but not without a bit of a struggle.

Major problem solved. Three more trips back into the culvert brought out five wiggly puppies. Mom had hollowed out a shallow den in the middle of the pipe and the bucket slipped over the tops of their heads with hardly a disturbed hair.

But surprise! As soon as we gave Mom the first of her pups, she commenced to lick and clean it as though nothing had happened. She even forgave us and became one of the nicest dogs a catcher could want. Mother love. Go figure.

So we took Mom and her pups into the kennel and booked her into Cage M. We left them together because Mom wanted it that way. Besides, the pups were just a bit too young to wean yet. But we hadn't counted on a story-book ending.

A couple of days later, Momma was identified by her former owner. No, not the most current one, the one before that. It was a young lady from the Children's home. A minor.

"Good deal," you say? Well, not quite, for there was a hitch in this git-a-long. Momma dog's previous owner was a teeny-bopper, a juvenile, who was under the authority of the State of Nevada, having been placed in a Children's home. She was a ward of the State and subject to the jurisdiction thereof. She was placed into the home when her natural parents were either unable or unwilling to care for her and she had to give away her beloved dog, the Momma dog in question, when she entered the home a few months earlier. It was just happenstance that she discovered her former pet at the pound. Momma dog apparently had not liked her interim home and just took off on her own. The girl knew nothing of it until she visited the kennel that day, which resulted in a grand reunion. Good timing!

You just gotta know that this story ends well. To make it short, there were a number of obstacles to overcome such as convincing the cottage parents, as they are known at the home, to allow her to accept not only the dog but the litter as well. Plus there was the problem of fines and fees which have to be accounted for in some fashion. You have to satisfy the auditors, you know, and they don't look at happy hearts, only numbers. So with a little push here and a little shove there, everything came together and Momma was reunited with her original owner. She gained a new home, a new set of owners and six or seven new caretakers at the cottage.

Not a bad day's work.

A PHOENIX DOG

*Oftentimes romance novels make reference to
someone who is or had been down and out as
'rising from their ashes like a Phoenix.' The
phrase is used figuratively for anything created
anew, after defeat, death or destruction. The
Phoenix analogy could be a concept,
representing hope.*

ACTUALLY, the Phoenix was a mythical bird which originated in ancient legend, an incarnation of the sun-god Ra. The bird was supposedly huge, characterized as having feathers of crimson and gold, a majestic and noble creature that lived for five hundred or more years. He was a lone bird, as no female Phoenix existed, therefore no offspring. When his allotted span of time elapsed, he took himself to his nest and ignited it and himself, creating his own funeral pyre. When all was reduced to ashes, he arose triumphant over death into a new life. And so, he arose time and time again in glory through the centuries, always from his own ashes.

I often wondered if the young man bound for the city of Phoenix that day knew of the legend, and if so, did he hope to renew his life in its environs.

A light sprinkling of snow had spotted the valley floor during the night, not the deep fluffy layer of white that poets envision, but rather more like a spotted and soiled blanket generally white but with dark blotches showing through here and there.

The blue and cloudless sky overhead banished all hopes of a truly white Christmas on the morrow. Working outside then, I was just putting the finishing touches to the dog runs during the morning's kennel-cleaning duties. The next step would be feeding and filling the water bowls for the few remaining dogs and cats at the Shelter. The season had been good to them as the adoption rate had been high and there were few animals left.

It was a better adoption season than the previous year had been, but not good enough. It is never good enough. We like to see them all adopted. Mankind is always wasteful, even of his pets, and leaves his leftovers behind. My thoughts were somber-gray that day.

I was roused from my doldrums when I heard "Excuse me, Sir" from a man on the other side of the fence. Maybe it was the "Sir" that did it. Good manners are such a rarity these days that even with my gray hair and silver badge I don't often get `sirred.'

I could not recall the young man's name as I turned to reply, but I knew well the voice and the face that had appeared at the Shelter daily in search of his lost dog. It had been going on for a full week. He had dropped by to tell me that this would be his last day in town, that he was even then on his way to Arizona, Phoenix to be exact, where he was to start a new job. He was not able to delay his departure any longer, although his beloved pet had not yet been found.

"Keep looking for my dog," he implored. "Keep looking. And when you find him, call me collect in Phoenix at this number, and I'll come back. Just call me!" He handed me a slip of paper through the fence and on it was a number in Phoenix and some descriptive notes about his dog.

I tried to assure him, quite honestly, that I would indeed do my best. But I knew that my best might not be good enough. How long can you remember a dog that you have never seen? I knew that the dog's image was clear in his mind, burned indelibly into his brain by the long association they shared. But to me the image was blurred: a large lump of love shaped like a German Shepherd but confused by a smattering of an ancestor that had jumped the fence. He had best be found soon or a hundred other dog shapes and faces would crowd him out. Unfortunately, he was not found.

The days passed, as days will do. Another cat refused to come down from another tree. Another dog lost. Another dog found. They often don't match up, these lost and found reports. Whatever happens to those lost ones that are never found again? A mystery, like the Bermuda Triangle or Big Foot. Where do they go?

I always suspect that the lost ones are warming someone else's heart somewhere.

A small private plane crashes while attempting to land. Survivors: two humans. Fatality: one dog. And more days go by.

Two dogs perish in a neighbor's slick-sided swimming pool. And more weeks pass until once again the snow dots the ground and imaginary sleigh bells ring in the distance.

Again, 'twas the night before Christmas. Actually, it was the day before and for the second year in a row I had Christmas duty at the kennel. We rotate the holidays so that the same person doesn't have to get stuck with the same holiday all the time. However, an employee had resigned on short notice and a replacement hadn't yet been hired so I was on duty again.

Oh well, I was nearly finished anyway and there was still plenty of day left. I was making a final check on the cage locks when one of the most chilling sounds a person can hear assailed my ears. It was that goshawful scream of squealing tires and burning brakes that precede a car crash. Instinctively I hunched my shoulders and braced for the impact but, blessedly, there was none. Surprised, I breathed more easily.

Turning, I watched as the car that had braked with such excessive zeal now made a wild U-turn and pulled to a stop at the door. Out hurtled a young man yelping excitedly.

"That's him! That's him!" he yelled, pointing to a German Shepherd in the nearby cage, one of the few pets remaining unclaimed in the shelter that day.

The big Shep, unlucky enough to have been unadopted, hit a lucky streak after all and he too, began to yelp excitedly. He had recognized his former owner, even after a year's separation, and I swear I saw copious tears in the eyes of both of them at their unexpected reunion.

Yes, it was the young man from Phoenix, home for the holidays. One full year after his dog disappeared, it had finally been found. It was truly Merry Christmas to all, and to all a good night!

I, for one, could not have received a finer Christmas present.

PUZZLE

Okay, let's have a show of hands. How many of you have ever seen, even once, a cat skeleton in a tree? Well, neither have I.

STILL, WHENEVER ONE OF THESE totally lovable but incredibly independent creatures gets up a tree, the phone at Animal Control never stops ringing. Everybody wants the cat down and they want it down now! Most everyone has ideas on how to do it but no volunteer ever offers to do it. They all want to confer the honor on someone else. Get a hook and ladder from the Fire Department. Call out the National Guard. Somebody do something!

People are smart. They want someone else to do it because they know it is downright stupid to go out on a limb no thicker than your wrist to rescue a perverse little critter that will only go up, up higher as you approach it.

"Rescue me," it says with a plaintive meow, then moves out of reach.

So the unlucky would-be rescuer goes up farther and farther until: SNAP! down comes the limb, down comes the party of the first part, said cat, and down comes the party of the second part, the rescuer. The big difference is that the cat will walk away from the incident with tail erect and confidence intact while the paramedics haul away the battered anatomy of the rescuing Good Samaritan.

That is why, as a general rule of thumb, Animal Control Officers will not go out on a limb to rescue a cat. Usually, the Fire Department and the utility companies will also decline the pleasure of effecting a rescue. So, what is to be done? Nothing is the usual, and best, answer. In due course, the cat will do exactly the opposite of what it did to get up there in the first place—climb on down of its own volition. Sometimes it takes a day or two for the marooned feline to work up the courage, and perhaps the appetite. But, they eventually do, and that is why you do not see cat skeletons festooning trees.

I will confess to climbing a tree or two, or gingerly inching my way across a rooftop in search of an elusive mouser. But more often than not, I just leave well enough alone for I know that it will do its own thing in its own good time, and do it quite well, thank you, without any human assistance.

I recall an incident that occurred several years ago when Momma cat had five or six of her little papooses in the bole of a giant cottonwood tree. The cottonwood is fairly common in the Nevada area and derives its name from the cotton-like seed it produces in white profusion. The tree has a rather high branch-less trunk for the first dozen feet of its height before it forks out, often with three or four major branches instead of just two. This branching effect creates a level, floored pocket which in turn provides an ideal nest so long as the weather is dry. Water will pool in the fork when it rains and provides a good birdbath but a lousy bedroom. Often, as the tree ages, this pooling will rot out the soft center of the tree and create a tunnel-like cavity in the trunk, sometimes several feet long.

It was in such a tree tunnel that Momma cat had her kittens. Naturally, her presence did not go unnoticed for long. That's when the phone at Animal Control went berserk. Try as we would, there was no convincing a group of good citizens that this was an A-OK arrangement and that Mom and kits would be fine.

So, lacking success in the area of convincing them, which was Plan A, I elected to try physical removal, which came under Plan B. I quickly discovered that by driving the van up against the tree and placing a ladder on the van roof, I could, from the top step of the ladder, reach up with a six-foot capture pole and hopefully chase them all down, one by one, from their rain tunnel refuge. But the little wizards wouldn't budge which, of course, totally defeated the value of Plan B, their rescue, and drove me back to Plan A, convincing.

This was clearly a job for astute public relations. I, if I do say so myself, conceived a diabolically clever plan. Standing atop the ladder precariously perched on top of the van, and reaching up as high as possible, I nailed a delectable opened tin of tuna to the tree. Thusly, I explained to the Doubting Thomases, it could be demonstrated by the empty tin that Momma was climbing down to the food and taking it, mouthful by mouthful, back to her waiting brood. Or, she could eat the tuna and in turn nurse the kits. Thus, I theorized, they would indeed be taken care of, with additional tins of tuna, and did not need any other type human intervention.

There now, doesn't that convince you? Well, it didn't convince those other concerned citizens either. For one thing, they couldn't see the interior of the can to see if the food was being eaten. Also, they feared that Mom would tip the can, spilling the contents on the ground and thus condemn the kittens to death by starvation.

What if squirrels ate the food, they questioned. The concerneds offered other reasons so logical and compelling that I cannot remember what they were. At any rate, they doubted my knowledge of felines as well as expertise in dealing with them and wondered if, indeed, I was playing with a full deck. And, most importantly, they wanted the kits down, down, down.

Since I was not going to go up, up, up to get the cats down, down, down, there had to be a more convincing demonstration that Mom could come and go as she pleased.

Came another brilliant solution. That evening, a nice, thick carpet of pure white pastry flour appeared all around the base of the tree. Sure enough, next morning, little kitty footprints appeared in the fresh white flour. Certainly, that ought to convince even the most cynical observer, I thought.

The rebuttal to this new proof was swift. It was obvious to everyone (but me) that Dad had come by to visit and had left his prints for all to see. Never mind that he must have been a midget to have feet so small. Mom and brood, they insisted, were still marooned in the tree. My finest strategies having been rejected, I was just a plain flat-footed failure in their eyes.

By this time, total desperation engulfed the situation. I was nearly ready to commit myself to the hazards of the climb. But, there was one more gambit to try.

I convinced them to sit with me every night, near the tree, for up to two hours per session, to observe the conduct of the feline family. We would put food on the ground at the base of the tree and wait to see what happened.

No one really wanted to do it but I was adamant and they reluctantly drew straws to see who would have the first watch. We would take up our station just at sunset to observe. The agreement was to watch until the weekend, and if Mom were not observed tending her flock, I was to go up the tree and, never mind the risk to my bones, get the cats down.

Boy, did I ever get lucky! On the very first night, Mom came out about nine o'clock and climbed down to the ground. After scouting the area but without touching the food, she raced back up the tree. In a moment or two she reappeared, brood in tow, and with gentle urging, brought the whole kit and caboodle down to the party. My reputation, and my bones, were saved.

But I must add this note: The incident occurred rather early in my career and I relied, in part, on advice I had received from so-called older and wiser heads. Since then, I have discovered only two instances where cats had perished in trees. In both cases, they had managed to wedge their torsos into a forked branch or trunk and, unfortunately, suffocated due to pressure on the lung cage before rescue could be put into effect.

So, overall, the best advice is still to give the cat the opportunity to come down on its own, unless it is obviously trapped. If the cat were somehow actually hung up in the tree and could not get loose, the safest way to get it down is to cut off the offending branch or limb and let it all fall. The cat will most likely jump clear without being injured. Of course, you may not see it again for a while or, if badly frightened by the incident, maybe forever.

SCHNITZEL

One of the most beloved veterinarians in Northern Nevada is a fellow by the name of Martin, Dr. William 'Bill' Martin.

BUT WHY IS HE SO REVERED? Mainly because he is the person responsible for my acquisition of Schnitzel. Before retirement he was what might be called a country vet. He had a Small Animal Practice, that is, dogs and cats, but he also handled livestock.

Doc likewise had a small airplane which he used to get to the far-out counties, the cow counties as they were called. He did a lot of ranch work and a lot of that required that he get there in a hurry. So he flew, piloting his own craft.

Like most folks do when getting close to retirement, Doc did a lot of thinking about how it would be. Originally he thought he would just laze around and do some fishing, hunting and such. So thinking, he allowed that he could use another dog and took on the responsibility of one. But once acquired, he changed his mind.

After all, he did have a pilot's license and an airplane to go with it, not to mention that he also had a lot of rancher type friends spread all over the state. All of that added up to a really good way to spend retirement. But what to do with the new dog?

Doc also had a few friends and acquaintances around town. The dog pound was on that list because we had done a lot of business with him over the years. So he asked us to pick up the dog and find a new home for it. He knew, as we do, that there are no guarantees when it comes to adoptions.

So he sweetened the deal. One year of free medical services for any of our animals' illnesses, all of the shots needed for good health including rabies vaccination and, best of all, free sterilization, namely a free spay job. Now that was a sweetheart deal and it convinced me that we could place this neat kid in a brand new home jet-quick.

The dog was a German Shepherd-Norwegian Elkhound mix of the female persuasion and she was flat-out beautiful. Now that's beautiful spelled with a capital B. She obviously had a sweet disposition and a ready wit and would be the hit of any party. A natural for adoption!

It was time to pull down that iron curtain that prohibits falling in love with an animal in the Shelter whenever undue emotion begins to cloud sober judgment. These are, after all, functions of the brain even though we tend to label them matters of the heart, so it's the job of the iron curtain to shield the brain before the heart gets involved.

It rarely works really well but it does help to keep the staff from catapulting head over heels with a prospective adoptee. More importantly, it gives warning that pain is at hand if failing to back off. The problem with a pet as perfect as Doc's is the certainty that an adoption is imminent if the curtain fails to fall. Bingo, it's hopeless love!

I had already fallen but my wife, Glenna, had not a clue except that she had been shown the dog on a couple of visits to the pound. I had made it a point to show this unique dog to her but I really did not have any Machiavellian schemes in mind at the time. This was not trickery. It was just that I knew this canine to be one of the prettiest and the best to come down the pike in a long, long time.

I had hesitated because I thought the rest of the world should have the opportunity to appreciate the facts. How could anyone resist such a marvelous pet as this? Especially when the good Doc had sweetened the pot so well? Suppose they called a war and nobody came?

Well, nobody came to this deal either. It was unthinkable to destroy such a magnificent animal. And I? I had failed to drop the iron curtain in time and I was hooked. The consequences of that failure meant that I had to step up to the plate and take my best swing at it. I adopted her and so began one of those relationships between human and animal that they write stories about.

We called her Schnitzel because she was German, which of course suggested *das wiener schnitzel*. In short order she became Nikki as well. Schnitzel? Nikki? Did Shakespeare have dogs in mind when he said "What's in a name?" Maybe so, for by any name this dog deserved remembrance. She will have it for as long as those of us who knew her draw a breath.

We all think that the grass is greener on the other side of the hill. If we have any amount of years behind us, we also know that after we climb up the hill, we are going to find that the grass is just exactly the same shade up close as it was from the bottom. Most of us therefore will not venture up the hill. At least not just to compare the color of the grass.

Every once in a while though, the temptation is just too great and off we go, trudging the long trail. Our trail led to the California coast. It was a good year in many ways. I reaped a harvest of rich experience working in a new environment with new people.

We took an apartment in the Napa wine country. During our stay there, we had the only large dog allowed on the premises. Very few apartments were leased to pet owners and all such had to be of the extremely small variety. Schnitzel was not extremely small. She was sort of extremely medium but due to my work and my assurances that we would vacate the instant anyone voiced legitimate complaint against my dog, we were allowed to take the apartment and keep Schnitzel there too.

I have loved many dogs. I love the ones I have now. But there is always one that stands out, one with a larger capacity for giving and receiving love than any other. That one stays with us forever. For me, that one was Schnitzel.

When we made the decision to go hill climbing and grass seeking, we had the granddaddy of garage sales and literally sold everything that would not fit into the trunk of the car. So once in Napa Valley, we had to go out and do the reverse. But we did buy a brand new sparkling clean living room set.

Nikki, AKA Schnitzel, was told politely but firmly that the couch was new and no longer a suitable place for dogs. Dogs belonged on the floor. People belonged on couches. The point was demonstrated a time or two and that was sufficient training for Nikki. I simply told her that I never wanted to catch her on the couch and she advised me that I never would. I never did.

What I did catch was a suspicious depression, a dog-sized declivity in the end pillow of the couch. Strangely enough, that particular pillow grew dog hair. None of the other pillows did, only the one on the end. When I came home from work, Nikki would be at the door, ready to greet me. Her eyes would be glowing and her ears were stretched tall and straight, eager to hear some praise from her master. I would glance at the suspicious pillow and look her straight in the eyes.

"Nikki, have you been on the couch?" I'd say. She would solemnly lower her eyes, her ears would droop back and down, and I'd swear she would shake her head no.

I vowed not to give in, not to relent. This was one battle I was going to win and I assured her that she would get spanked if I ever caught her on the couch. I didn't relent, and I never caught her. But I did find myself sitting on the floor beside her more often than ever before.

Eventually the grass turned brown and we returned to Nevada. When we got back vacant domains were scarce and there was not a place to be found that would allow us to keep Schnitzel. We tried, believe me, we tried. We turned down several lovely places because of the 'no pets' rules. Finally, after several weeks of failures and with our savings running low, we were forced to make that awful decision. It was my beloved friend, the dog, or us.

I had failed not only in my search for a home that would allow us to keep Schnitzel but also failed to find a home that would keep her for me. That left me with but two options: One, have her destroyed; and two, find a new home for her, one that would not, could not, include me.

I started to take her daily to the kennel knowing that she would get the best possible public exposure there. I could not, would not, consider option number one. A new home would, in many ways, be just as painful to me but at least she would be alive and, I hoped, happy.

A curious incident occurred one day, and Nikki was spared. A young lady came into the kennel looking for her lost dog, rather desperately looking and hoping. You could tell that she felt deeply about her loss.

As the fates would have it, her pet was there. It didn't take too long to arrange the paperwork and pay the impound fines and as we walked back into the kennel she let out a cry of dismay. We had entered through a different door this time. Just inside the door, in Kennel #13, sat her second dog. She hadn't mentioned the loss of this dog because she figured, erroneously, that it could not be caught as it was a skilled escape artist.

I had already sized her, so to speak, so I knew that she was an animal lover and that any animal placed in her care would be in good hands. Simply put, I would pay her adoption fees and she could take both of her friends home if, in addition, she would acquire one new friend, Nikki. My only conditions were that I be allowed two follow-up visits. It was not out of concern that she would not take care of Nikki. It was out of my selfish concern that Nikki had adjusted to her new home.

She agreed and the deed was soon done. It was, at one and the same time, the brightest and the blackest deed I'd ever done to myself.

The allotted two visits assured me, calmed me. Schnitzel was happy with her new mistress. As I left her new home after my second visit, a feeling of overwhelming loss filled me with grief. I truly loved that dog. She was 'family,' and life would not be the same without her. She was gone. Life went on.

ONE DAY AT THE OFFICE a call came in for me, personally. This was not too unusual since the town is somewhat small, compared to a metropolis, that is, and after a while everyone gets to know everyone else.

Nevertheless we always try to screen calls and have the office staff handle them except when it appears that the call should go directly to the officer involved in a particular case or situation.

Thus the staff is better equipped to keep accurate call records and process any paperwork generated by the call. It is more efficient that way since we officer types are not really good at paperwork anyway.

But this was a call that was directed to the person involved, namely me. Our office manager had already clued me in as to who was calling so I was not surprised when Julie started to talk as soon as I got on the line. Her husband, Skip, was on the extension so I was soon talking to both of them. The story they were telling me was about a stray dog that needed me to come and pick it up at their house.

I was busy doing something or other at the time and so I told them "No problem. I'll have Mack pick it up." Mack was already out doing field work and it was reasonable to just pass the pick-up on to him.

However, Skip and Julie would simply not hear of it. They insisted that it was something that I had to do and they gave me some goofy reason for it. I figured they just wanted to shoot the breeze for a while and I knew I could cut the conversation short so I agreed to do it.

My van had barely braked to a stop in their driveway when they both came out to meet me. They seemed nervous or something—different in a way I could not quite equate with the phone call. I supposed that maybe they were feeling a little silly about insisting that I make this call personally. I was also a little surprised that they did not have the vagrant dog tied up in front of the house. Julie and Skip both love dogs and since they had Prince in the house, I wondered why the pick-up dog would be inside too since it didn't seem prudent to take another dog in with Prince who was half moose and half St. Bernard and it was problematical which half would greet any strange dog.

They opened the door and waved me inside in front of them. There was still no dog inside except for Prince, who promptly set me back on my heels with his greeting. Prince likes me. And when Prince likes you, he wants to greet you properly according to his fashion, which is to stand on hind legs and plant one each of his giant front paws on each of your shoulders and then plant a big wet kiss on any part of your face that you do not get out of the way fast enough. You have to brace yourself for this onslaught of affection or go down on your behind. Your choice.

After being appropriately greeted by Prince I inquired as to where the other dog was. It was time to get crackin'.

They informed me that they had put the dog in the spare bedroom. Now the spare bedroom at Skip and Julie's was a room down the hall that receives anything and everything that doesn't fit somewhere else in the house. To even call it a bedroom is a joke. Yes, it had a bed which was under a bunch of stored stuff. It was a catch-all room, more closet than anything else.

I started down the hallway and Skip and Julie fell in behind me, walking in lock step, single file like soldiers on parade. I felt like I was being tailgated.

I stopped and, turning partially around, inquired as to what was going on. I could have sworn I saw two hastily removed grins on their faces but they blandly explained that they just wanted to see how I would handle the stray dog, being a professional and all. Whatever floats your boat, thinks I, but come on anyway. So we proceeded to the closed spare bedroom door with the two of them in close tow.

I opened the door and for a long moment I forgot to draw a breath as time stood still. There, in front of me, bright-eyed and bushy-tailed, was my relinquished Schnitzel, she having been mandatorially given away when the green grass turned brown and we returned to Nevada and could find no dwelling that would accommodate her.

Her ears were erect and her eyes were alight with that happy glow I knew so well. Tears dimmed my eyes and I was rendered stone-stiff for a moment. I could not react. I could not even move.

Nikki's ears began to droop as they always did whenever I expressed dissatisfaction. She, in her canine mind, took my lack of response as a sign of displeasure and her barometer, her ears, began to fall.

It was her reaction, her sensitivity to my mood that finally broke the spell.

With a whoop and a holler, I had her in my arms once again, trying to pet and talk to her all at once. She was busy trying to greet me. We yelled and whined and rolled on the floor and generally made fools of ourselves. I did the worst job of it because dogs are supposed to act that way but humans are supposed to be more dignified.

Now I knew the answer to Skip's and Julie's behavior for even though they had never laid eyes on Schnitzel before that day, they knew her to be mine, and they reunited us. How could that have happened?

Faced with having to give Schnitzel away, I had been lucky enough to meet that wonderful lady who took Nikki in. She however, had encountered hard times and in the process of getting out of them received a job opportunity too good to turn down. But it was in Alaska, and she could only take two critters with her. She naturally chose to take her own two dogs.

She was busy looking for a way out when she ran into Skip and Julie. It was a fluky meeting. She was selling most everything she owned and had a yard sale for that purpose. Skip and Julie were garage sale junkies and showed up for the event. The good lady noticed that moose-sized Prince was in the back seat of the car and commented on the fact that 'they must be big dog people.' Dog people talk about dogs and one thing led to another and pretty soon the good lady offered a dog to them because she could not take it with her. They advised her to talk to 'Lee' at the pound and see if he could help and she responded with the comment that 'she could not do that' and repeated the offer a couple more times and again was advised to 'call Lee.'

Finally, she explained that she could not do that because she had made a promise and a commitment to Lee and this had been his dog and she couldn't face him.

That's when Skip and Julie looked at each other and in that silent way people have when they knew each other well, agreed to take the dog. For me.

And that, in Paul Harvey tradition, is the end of the story.

ASSIGNED, SEALED AND DELIVERED

*I knew all too well what that strange sucking
sound was. It was confirmation that my right foot
was rapidly sinking deeper into the tidal muck as
I stepped off the pier into the shallow water
where the monster sloshed around frantically. I
didn't like it there.*

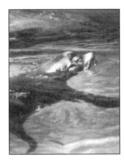

WHEN I JOINED THE OUTFIT on the West
Coast, I had visions of merely capturing stray
dogs, writing a citation or two, and spending
a lot of time on patrol. Patrol is that routine
of your employment where you drive around
the residential and business districts of your
assigned territory and look for conditions
that might be amiss. Usually it is fairly
uneventful and you tend to get accustomed to
the routine. Except for cases like this.

The critter in front of my rapidly disappearing foot had some
really impressive canine type teeth and an awesome bark but he,
or maybe she, was certainly no dog. How did I get into this mess
anyway? I hadn't bargained for it, that's for sure.

It started when the Marine Institute called us for backup. It
seems that they did not have enough available manpower for
the job at hand and they figured someone qualified with animals would do just as well as a marine biologist could. Hence
my presence.

The logic was a bit twisted but it made ultimate sense, as in some cases, a little experience is better than none. That part was right. I knew, at least, which end of the floundering mammal had teeth.

I had always thought that ocean waves came in and ocean waves went out. In the process there was a kind of sweeping action which I thought always cleansed the shoreline. Nay, not so. The stuff I was standing in was primordial ooze, the kind of yucky slime that first saw life aeons ago in its timeless procession to the present. Apparently the waves did come in and out, but the stuff the waves carried in stayed put. All of it was old and most of it stunk. I was more than ready to leave but dogcatchers all over the world were counting on me to not conk out. I had to stay.

There was some kind of exotic virus going around the community, it seems, and this critter obviously had contracted a severe case of it and needed rescue in order to recover and not spread the infection farther. It was obvious he was not in a charitable mood.

The marine biologists had determined the sexual proclivities of this guy, and I soon figured out that he was a rather *large* bull seal. Hence the vicious bark. His affliction was upper respiratory, the bios said, and was fatal if not treated. The disease was carried by microorganisms in the water. I again pondered the fate of my rapidly sinking leg, assuming of course, that I would eventually get it back.

The episode turned out to be rather simple after all. The two marines (I had begun to think of them that way. You know, a couple of good men) captured the tooth end of the fractious bull, and I backed them up. We slipped, slithered and slopped and finally managed to get a large and quite heavy fish net around him.

The net was not unlike a hammock and quite immobilized the seal once we got it on. The marines were also careful not to get bitten because, they said, there are few bites more infectious than seal bites. Rotten fish and all that, don't you know.

None of us came away dry because a seal is like a long muscle with slappy flippers and this one had managed to easily catch us off balance and knock us into the cold water. Nor did any of us fail to reek of salt water slime.

A follow-up call a few days later assured me that the rescue was successful. The seal had responded favorably to the antibiotics he received and was once again back home in the briny deep.

And yes, I did get my leg back, intact.

"...it's an old trick I learned at
my grandfather's fin..."

RESCUES AWRY

Oftentimes animals in apparent distress do not need to be rescued at all. They just need to be left alone to do their own thing in their own good time. But just as often, we the people, do not leave well enough alone and actually interfere with the process.

THE TINY LITTLE RACCOON hugged the slender tree branch with all the strength his baby paws could muster. The foothill winds, straight off the High Sierra, were gusting at a mere 60 miles per hour and whipped the little fellow's perch back and forth in a thirty degree arc. It's a wonder he didn't get seasick from the seesaw he was on.

That in itself was my good fortune because he might have barfed all over me as I was standing on terra firma just under his precarious perch. It was fairly obvious that the best thing I could do for him was to merely go away and leave him alone. The winds wouldn't hurt him and the Great Dane that had put him up there in the first place had been moved to another yard a significant distance away so as to allow the coon a degree of comfort. It offered sufficient leeway for him to venture down whenever he felt the need.

That was an if-and-when proposition but he would do so when he felt conditions were right. *He* would make the decision. What he needed was to be left alone to work out his own destiny.

TV IS GREAT STUFF. It provides both fact and fantasy for millions of viewers every day. The only problem is that it is sometimes hard to separate one from the other. Where does fact stop and fantasy begin?

One of the most popular types TV fare is any show that relates to animals, any animal, doing anything at all, or just sitting there twitching. Animals are frequently used as background in TV commercials because they lend an aura of comfort.

Because animals do this job so well, rescue societies use them to promote contributions. One of the most common practices in this promotional effort is to show some of the abuses animals suffer such as abandonment, neglect or cruel usage of equipment. Those are effective messages, although a bit on the depressing side, so another tack is often used, that is, the rescue scene.

An animal gets into big trouble and the savior society charges to the rescue. Their efforts are applauded. There is, however, another side to these stories. It is a funny side—examples of rescue attempts that went all wrong. But since the animals involved suffered no harm, documentation of the abortive attempts are worth a chuckle or two.

THERE WAS THIS DUCK that lived in a public park on a big man-made lake. He was a mallard, one of many that cut short their southern migration and just stayed put. His lake, like a lot of others built in public parks, was regularly stocked with a variety of small fishes tempting little folks to try their piscatorial luck. Big people, also known as adults, are not allowed to fish there. It's strictly kid stuff. It is really great fun for the little tots and is educational as well.

But there is a darker side to the process: fish hooks and fish lines that are no longer attached to fishing poles which, in turn are supposed to be attached to little people but aren't. Most communities that sponsor such programs have learned to restrict the types lures, hooks and lines that the kids are allowed to use.

The small hooks and light lines permitted generally do not present a threat to the ducks, geese, swans and other waterfowl that frequent those safe havens. Usually the little hooks will rust and break off a duck's bill in short order and without harm. And the lines that entangle feet break off just as easily. Sometimes however, the lines will get a bird so tangled that it can neither walk, swim nor fly. A bird is in trouble when it can't do any of those locomotive things.

And that is what happened to The Mallard. He was so fouled up that he could barely paddle in the water, let alone waddle on land. And he couldn't get airborne either, not with tangled feet. To make things worse, his starboard paddle was better than his port side paddle so that when he did exert the effort, he would go around in circles only: one-way circles, around and around and around in the middle of the pond.

Society to the rescue: boat, oars, net, long pole with loop, officers. Yep, all set to go. But wait! There is no camera or camcorder to record the event. That state of affairs is simply unthinkable in relation to agency publicity, hence fund-raising! So what to do?

Well, the quickest answer is to call the local news media and let the professionals film it for maximum TV coverage on the evening news. That way kills two birds with one shot: live coverage and a video for later. What could be better? And so the march of history in the making is stilled while waiting for the media to appear and make it an event.

Meanwhile, poor Mr. Mallard was getting pretty tired of circulating in the middle of the lake and he did what ducks will do under those circumstances. He rolled over, belly up. He might even have drowned had not some bright and energetic kid sized up the situation and did what needed doing. He quickly stripped to skivvies and plunged into the lake. He swam out and rescued Mr. Mallard without benefit of TV coverage.

Thus it was all over. The lines were cut and both the port and starboard paddles were freed up and the mallard paddled happily away in a straight line, all the while quacking as though he had done something great himself. Since he was no longer going around in circles, he was of no interest to the press when they finally arrived.

OR, THERE WAS THIS lady type feline, almost a kitten but not quite, that found itself up a tree. It was in reality a rather short tree, as trees go. The cat-kitty was rather more not in danger than endangered. However, the particular spot in which the tree grew and the way it was positioned as against the rest of the terrain had all the makings of a spectacular photo.

Picture this: the little tree was on the cusp of a dry wash, so much so that a portion of the tree's root system was actually in the wash.

Now, if a person with a camera were to stand in the bottom of the wash just below the exposed root system and look up toward the tree, it would indeed look like a very tall, tall tree. Likewise the cat-kitten in the tree would appear to be caught 'way up high in a very tall, tall tree. Naturally, anyone in the tree stretching out a friendly hand to the stranded kitty would also seem to be 'way up high in a tall, tall tree. A perfect publicity shot!

Actually, the rescuer would in fact be just a few feet off the ground but with the right camera angle: Wow! What a great shot it would make. It was a moment too good to pass up. Just think of the funds that could be raised with that one!

With artful precision, an officer poised, hand outstretched toward the hapless cat-kitty away up high in the really rather short tree. Another gent got positioned in the bottom of the wash and maneuvered to get just the right camera angle.

Ahhh, the best-laid plans of meece and man! A rock beneath the foot, some loose soil, a shifting of weight and the cameraman went south. The noise of the falling body alarmed the feline that, ignoring the outstretched hand of salvation, leaped nimbly to the ground and rescued herself.

Photo op farewell!

YOU KEEP THE VOLVO

The complaint came in as a welfare checkout on a black Labrador Retriever. It originated from a woman who claimed that her ex-husband was not feeding the animal and was otherwise neglecting it. The 'ex' in front of 'husband' was a clue that this was perhaps more of a harassment call than a welfare review. Nevertheless, it had to be investigated.

THE HOME ON THE PRETENTIOUS WEST SIDE was of field stone and was constructed in English Tudor design. It was a modest place of some thirty thousand square feet, give or take a few, with three floors and more garages than most hotels. I didn't get to go inside as even the servants' door was closed to the likes of me.

The dog's quarters adjoined the main house and were finished in the same style architecture at the main dwelling. The principal difference was that the doors and windows were open spaces and it was only one story high. A stout link fence delineated the dog's pen which had a concrete base in lieu of grass, excepting for a sandy portion that was probably the loo, as the English are prone to say. I could not imagine that the dog was suffering much from what I could see. He was not inside the pen at that moment so I could only judge by the amenities I observed from the driveway.

I touched the front bell and chimes played from deep inside the house. After a long wait, someone made her way to the front door. She probably could not readily find the golf cart and had to walk the whole way to answer the door, which would explain the long delay.

A young lady of preteen persuasion greeted me, politely but curiously. She was accompanied by a striking specimen of Labrador. Quick surveyal of both of them convinced me that I need look no further into allegations of neglect. Since all of us in Animal Control are loathe to delve into legal issues with a minor, I simply asked her to give her father my card and have him call me when he returned home. She demurely responded that she would do so.

The rest of the story is of no account whatever except to illustrate what can sometimes happen in divorce cases. The family pet can play an important part in the settlement, as much as the family car or even the home itself. Judges are thus often reluctant to get involved in the dispute over this form of property since the owners usually do not regard the pet as chattel even though the law must do so, albeit with reservations.

It would be easy if the disagreement were over a TV set or such. Just buy another one of equal value and have done with the issue.

But a pet is a unique possession since there is no other quite like it. Sure, just find another Lab, but it would not be the same. It is the personal relationship with the animal that is crucial. It approximates the argument over cloning. One living thing is not like another, in spite of the most striking similarities. And so, getting another dog does not even the score. Nor can the Solomon routine prevail. Cutting a Lab in half doesn't work.

The most sensible approach is to settle the issue before the separation or divorce. I have seen this done just as though the pet were a human child. One party gets custody and the other gets visitation rights. It happens.

Part of the success of this arrangement is due to the nature of modern society which has distanced itself somewhat from the closeness of community that used to prevail in America. The family unit is smaller and less likely to have extended ties with other relatives and is, at the same time, more mobile. Hence the suburban community ties are lessened and the immediate family ties are strengthened. The family pet is thus often the pawn in that condensed unity and a divorce has to embody the pet as well as family members.

For me, I'll just wish you a long and happy marriage and if it goes kaput, please keep me out of the middle. Thank you.

"No way!! I get the car and you get the cat!
I got a cat last time!"

YOU KEEP THE VOLVO

THE RIBWALKERS

Was it that one of us was clever and one was not?
Or was it just that one was more inquisitive and
possessed a more vigorous approach to learning
about new things?

AT ANY RATE, only one of us Golden Retrievers went after the thing hiding behind the tools and boxes in the storage shed. It seemed harmless enough. It wasn't very big and it had little tiny teeth and that wiggly fang that you could barely feel when it bit you. The pain came later.

It was quick though, like a boxer's left jab when its head popped out and tapped you on the nose and was gone before you could catch it. This was really great fun and was a much better thing to bark at than falling leaves or wailing sirens. It even flinched when you got off a particularly good bark right in its face.

It was all such a blast that it was mystifying when Grandma came out to investigate the commotion and got all upset, almost hysterical. She hadn't acted this bad since I chased Aunt Sophie's silly little poodle under the back porch where all the spiders lived. If anything, this was worse, she said. She made me quit and took both of us into the house and started calling people on that telephone thing.

It wasn't very long before a stranger drove up to the house and started talking to her and looking at me. I could tell that I was in trouble but I didn't think I had done anything wrong.

But I didn't feel so good any more, either. My nose was itching and starting to burn a lot and I felt kinda out of place. My head wasn't working too good either. I heard the man say it could kill me and that he would take me in the big white van if Mom's car was too small.

Anyway, that's what happened and he took me some place where they did things to me and I got better. Funny thing though, every place where that little thing with the tiny fangs bit me turned black and all the hair around it fell off. I had big bald spots all over my face.

AND THAT IS WHAT IT'S LIKE, if you are a dog, to be bitten by a rattlesnake. Generally, so they say, a rattlesnake bite won't kill you but many a dog has found out otherwise.

For one thing, those that are smaller, hence less body mass, mean more poison per pound. Add the fact that the bites are almost always in the face, that is, closer to the brain, and the equation starts to get dangerous.

Finally, dogs, thinking as the Golden did, that this is all just a fun thing, get bitten more often. The sum total is that a snakebite can cause an agonizing kill, and often does, when the victim is a dog.

It is likely that this particular dog would have been a fatality if it had not gotten to a vet in time.

The rattlesnake is a pit viper and is characteristically identified by the pits on either side of its head by the eyes. And of course, it is better recognized by the rattles which are formed by shedding its skin two or three times a year. Most people think that rattlers should be avoided at all cost and we in Animal Control agree. We only handle them when their presence is apt to be a danger to people or pets.

Ever since Eve was tempted by the snake in the Garden, most people would prefer that they simply abscond. Actually, while some of them may be dangerous, most snakes are generally beneficial in their consumption of rodents and insects, which helps to maintain ecological balance. It's just that they have a certain mystique that causes a high degree of repugnant abhorrence.

IT WAS SOMEWHAT THE SAME with that six-foot long boa constrictor curled up beneath a car in the supermarket parking lot. Onlookers were repulsed but fascinated. Most of the people gathered around ooohed and aaahed but kept their distance.

It was a cool spring day and the snake at the market was enjoying the heat from the asphalt and seemed disinclined to go anywhere. One enterprising fellow actually picked it up and held it for us. He had owned exotic snakes before and knew the hows and whys of snake handling. That made it possible for us to simply collect all six feet of reptile and take it to the shelter to wait and see what would happen next.

The conclusion wasn't long in coming. The snake's owner was moving to another county and had just stopped briefly at the market. The snake somehow escaped the car and took a hike, that's all.

While snakes are generally rather slow moving creatures, not many people are willing to race them. One African reptile has been clocked at about seven miles per hour. That's about twice as fast as a brisk morning walk and more than fast enough if you are trying to evade a reptile.

There are some 2,000 varieties of snakes around the world and they range in size from about six inches to over thirty feet. With that many different ones around, it is no wonder that we usually just say "Duh?" when asked what kind of snake it is that someone has found somewhere. Who could identify them all?

Snakes crawl around on the ground by swinging their bodies in loops from side to side, aided by up to 300 pairs of cartilage ribs which are articulated and joined by muscles so as to allow them to move in a fashion similar to legs without joints, stiff-legged as it were. Thus, they literally 'walk' on their ribs. The sidewinder has a peculiar sidewise movement which seems to propel him as much to the side as to the front.

Animal Control catches snakes using two different methods. The easiest way to capture a nonvenomous reptile is to roll a round stick, such as a broom handle, up the snake's back to just behind the head and then press the snake into the ground. Holding it captive in that manner, it is possible to then reach up and grasp the snake just behind the head. It will usually coil around the capturing arm but won't injure the captor. It is amazing to experience the power in the grip that even a small snake can exert in this position. It is reminiscent of the arm cuffs that nurses use when taking blood pressure. It is that sort of constriction.

The same method can be used when picking up poisonous snakes but being prudent myself, I prefer using the recommended snake tongs. That is a tool similar to kitchen tongs but with a longer handle. With tongs the snake can be grasped behind the head and picked up without using hands or injuring the snake.

The next step is then to put it into some kind of container. Most Animal Control Officers use a pillow case for emergency transportation. Simply put the snake in the case by inserting the whole reptile inside the open end, letting it go and then shaking it down while tying a string around the top. Satin pillow cases are best because the snake cannot 'get a grip' on the slick surface.

But it takes a special type individual to advance beyond repugnance and recognize the biological beauty of reptiles.

Bravado? Anyone?

"...and so when he reaches in
for us I'll say, 'His-s-s-s' and you go
'Rattle...rattle...rattle...'."

BIRD IN A GILDED CAGE

*The glass-sided towers were each taller than any
of the buildings enclosed within their perimeter.
Thus they looked down on not only the grounds
but also on the rooftops. Each tower was linked
to all of the other towers by radio, by telephone
and by line-of-sight. Nothing could venture in or
out, day or night, without being observed. My van
was parked well outside the perimeter and did
not have to be searched.*

 **I, ON THE OTHER HAND,** would be going in
through the triple-doored entry and was
therefore required to relinquish anything on
my person that was made of metal. The
detector didn't beep when I passed through it.
Soon I was in the maximum security prison
and flanked by a prison guard. My entrance
had been announced to each of the guard
towers. I knew why I was there and I hoped it
was worth the trip. This was not a particularly
nice place to visit.

At one time it was a leisure mecca. Then it was a gathering
place for city notables since it contained warm water springs and
a hotel. It was said that the elected representatives of the capital
city of Nevada gathered there for libation and other relaxations. I
wouldn't know, for that was well before my time, but I was sure I
would have preferred it then.

Several involuntary occupants of the quarters gave me a curious once-over, having spotted my ID insignia, wondering of course why I was there since there were no dogs running loose around the compound. Actually, I was called because a bird needed rescuing from the cage of bars, wire and guns.

It was a bird of prey and was a member of the family tree which claims eagles and ospreys. It was a red-tailed hawk that had somehow found itself in an unusual predicament. It had probably dived into its unplanned cage in pursuit of lunch, or dinner. Even though hawks have eyesight roughly eight times sharper than that of humans, it could have been that it did not see the shiny razor wire that would ensnare it. Or maybe it just could not unfold its wings sufficiently to fly out, once trapped. Whatever, it was in need of rescue and none of the prison guards felt up to the challenge.

Hawks have hooked beaks that are used to rend their prey helpless, and even though they are a small specie of bird, they can inflict painful wounds. Their powerful talons can likewise do considerable damage. That's the reason falconers wear leather gauntlets to catch their birds upon retrieval. Surveying the hawk through its gleaming cage, I wasn't sure I was up to the challenge either.

It turned out to be a fairly easy capture since the bird was confined in that shiny looping roll of wire on top of the brick wall which divided a terraced area from the main yard in which several guests played ball, lifted weights and otherwise diverted their attention from the humdrum.

One of the guards had thoughtfully provided me with a long ladder, usually kept not only under lock and key but outside the walls. I was then able to reach through a loop of the razor wire and net the hawk. Once so restrained, a bird can be held down and grasped safely around the body from the back, thus immobilizing its wings. Also grasping the bird up high toward the neck prevents it from turning around to attack. I had a carrier ready to go and the hawk was soon inside so we could both make an exit.

I took it for a checkup to a bird expert who maintains a sanctuary in the next county. This lady should be nominated for sainthood inasmuch as she runs an operation that has saved the lives of thousands of winged creatures. It turned out that this one was not injured or in need of repair and it was soon released and soaring to the winds again.

I WILL ADMIT TO having received a fowl's bite or two along the animal control pathway. I think the most unlikely nosh was by a seagull. He had been dragging one wing and needed a bit of help. Most likely he had hit a power line while in flight and had slightly torqued one wing.

Gulls will usually recover from such a nonserious injury but they do need to be put somewhere safe until recovery. The local sanitary landfill is generally a haven for such injured fowl as there is always plenty of scavenge around until flight is again possible.

So, while attempting to pick up the seagull, it bit me. Gulls have a little tooth-like tip on the top beak and that accoutrement is sharp—and usually dirty. That's what got me, and even with a disinfectant wash, the bite sparked infection.

AS FOR BIRDS OF A FEATHER, I am reminded of the time that I went to California to consult with a fellow officer about some problems we shared in common even though we operated in different states. I was stopped on the street by a woman, rather small in stature, actually quite petite, but who seemed to have a problem larger than herself. She frowned and seemed reluctant to approach but did so anyway, timidly. She was looking at my uniform.

"Pardon me. You're not a police officer, are you?" she ventured, hesitantly.

"No. Do you need a police officer?" I asked.

"I don't know," she replied, uncertainty strong in her otherwise timid tone. I wondered where this scintillating conversation was going. It was anybody's guess at this point.

"What's the problem?" I bothered to inquire. And that was my first mistake.

"I hear voices," she said helplessly.

Oboy. Time to bail out. Feet don't let me down. But she was too quick.

"Yes," she said, brightening a bit that somebody was listening to her tale. "Every time I go out into my back yard I hear voices."

I wanted to suggest that she stay out of her back yard as it was obviously haunted but she continued right on as though I didn't have a response in my head.

"I don't think I'm crazy," she lamented, "but I need to convince my husband that I'm not."

I started to back away gracefully while explaining that psychiatry wasn't exactly my calling but she was again too quick and I didn't have a chance.

"I was out in the back yard," she repeated, "which is quite large. Suddenly I heard a raspy voice that said, real nasty like, 'Out of my way, creep!' We'd had a prowler a few weeks before and I thought maybe somebody was hiding in the bushes. That's when I ran inside, real fast."

"Thing to do," I agreed and again turned to flee. But she tugged at my sleeve, an implied and not too subtle bid to hear more of what she had to say.

"I started to call the police," she went on, "but first I watched the yard from a back window but I didn't see anybody so I would have felt silly calling them, y'see."

I saw, and sympathized with her husband.

"Did you ever find out who it was?" I asked as I lent her my empathetic ear for the moment.

"Well no," she continued. "But the next morning I went outside again and I heard that same awful voice. 'Scram, crumbum!' it said, and I did. And while I was running back into the house that fresh scoundrel had the audacity to yell, real sarcastic-like, 'Tootle-ooo!' Such nerve! Whoever it was had all the birds upset too. There was a lot of screeching going on in the big old trees overhead."

"Hmmm," I said, and turned to go. But she ignored the effort.

"I told my husband about it and he just said, 'You're nuts. You been drinkin'? You better git yourself over to AA.' That was an insult because I don't drink." She seemed to be genuinely distressed.

How did I get myself into this mess? But I had an out.

"This is not in my territory," I explained, meaning both territorially and psychologically, which gave me a good excuse to turn away and leave. But she interrupted again.

"You got a piece of paper?" she asked, obviously seeing a small notebook protruding from my jacket pocket. I tore off a blank sheet and gave it to her.

"Your pen?" she motioned to the pen also clipped beside it. Then she scribbled something on it and gave them both back to me.

"Here's my name and address," she said. "Maybe if you have time you could come look at my back yard?"

"Maybe," I agreed. Anything to get out of the zany situation. In return she heaved a big sigh. "Thanks," she said, seemingly much relieved, and turned to go.

I glanced at the scribbled address. It was a street I knew well. Then I took refuge in a handy coffee shop, wadding up the little slip of paper as I took a seat at the counter.

"Coffee?" the waitress asked as she placed a cup of the steaming brew in front of me before I even had a chance to answer. Being the efficient sort, she also wiped off the counter and whisked away the crumbled note.

That's when the long arm of flukes reached out. Sitting at the counter a couple of stools away were two elderly gents talking loud enough to make it easy to eavesdrop on their conversation.

"What are they gonna to do about all them parrots down in the park?" one of them said.

"Nuthin' I guess," his companion replied in a raspy croak. "What can they do? Boids is boids."

I simply had to jump on this.

"You have parrots around here?" I inquired.

"Yeah, down in that little park off of Sixth Street. It seems somebody a couple of decades ago had a pair of parrots that got away and they settled down in the park where they raised a big family and now they're jabberin' and screamin' all day long. Besides, they make big messes on our dominoes tables."

Eureka! That made sense since parrots are known to live for fifty years and longer. And, remembering the street of the lady in distress, it was apparent she lived just up the hill from the park. But what was her house number? It was, of course, scribbled on that scrap of paper the waitress had snatched.

"Pardon me, Miss," I called to her. "You picked up a little wad of paper a minute ago?"

"Yeah," she nodded.

"Could I have it back?" I dared ask.

"I'd have to dig in the garbage for it," she said, sounding not too enthusiastic.

"But I need it," I insisted. She scowled and went away, returning with it in a few minutes, the note slightly messy but otherwise intact. I gulped down my coffee and left her a buck tip for what was, in that era, a 15-cent cup of java.

I now felt the least I could do was inform that disturbed little lady she was quite sane and that she had probably just heard some parrots in her back yard. Needless to say she welcomed the news when I rang the bell.

"You'll tell my husband, won't you?" she pleaded.

I really didn't want to get involved in the marriage counselor business but I figured what the heck, I'd come this far. I would tell the little ole guy that his wife wasn't nuts. I was ill-prepared for the big burly bruiser that she brought to the front door—a brash know-it-all, no-nonsense guy.

"Yeah. What d'ya want?" he barked. I could see why she might be intimidated by him. It was obvious he considered me an intruder but my uniform lent a hint of authority, so he tolerated my presence.

"I'm just informing residents of your area," I fibbed, "that if you hear any strange conversations out in your yard, it's probably just some escaped parrots that are roosting down in the park."

"Parrots, eh? Well, I'll be damned!" And he looked at his tiny little wife in shocked curiosity, surprised to discover that maybe she was intelligent after all.

She just grinned. From ear to ear. I could also see her giving him an impulsive I-told-you-so glare.

And to me she gave the OK sign, and a knowing he-just-*thinks*-he's-the-boss shrug, with a wink toward her retreating husband.

"Tootle-ooo," she chortled as I turned to finally make that planned exit.

Some days it's easier to capture vicious dogs.

"Is that all you have to say for yourself?
'Nevermore...Nevermore...'?"

CLYDE, THE WOLF-DOG

*What kind of dog do you think of when it is
named Clyde? I'll give you two-to-one odds that
you come up with a deep South hill-country dog
such as a blue tick hound or a sad-eyed, droopy-
eared Basset.*

CLYDE IS A GOOD NAME for a hound dog. It just seems to fit. I
have known a couple of Clydes that belong to the hound family. I
also once knew two Pit Bulls, one of them named Clyde, but not
for hound dog reasons. The other one was named Bonnie and
they earned that combination for appropriate reasons. They tried
to emulate the infamous pair of criminals of the same name
and did achieve the same unsavory reputation. They were not a
nice pair.

The Clyde that sticks best in my memory is no kind of
hound. Nor is he sad-eyed or droopy-eared. Awe-inspiring is a
more apt description of both his appearance and his conduct. I'm
glad that Kujo came on the scene after I met Clyde because if I had
seen the movie or read the book beforehand, I would never have
gotten out of the truck that day.

Nell, my fellow officer, was doing routine patrol when she
first spotted Clyde and a companion dog on the street. Nell was
our newest officer, but an old hand in the business.

When she spotted the twosome, she pulled over to the wrong
side of the street in order to put the van closer to where the dogs
were. That put the driver's seat next to the curb and naturally, put
Nell closer as well.

One of the dogs was a big guy and the other was about medium size, probably a Labrador mix. The big one seemed to be in charge and watched Nell's maneuver with apparent interest but not with a great deal of evident concern. His name was Clyde but Nell had no way of knowing that at the time. He certainly did not look like a Clyde.

He watched Nell get out of the truck and his interest in her rose with that action. It seemed he did not like the idea too well for he turned to face her squarely and this could have given her a clue to the dog's temperament.

Nell was now fully out of the truck and took a few steps toward the dogs while keeping a wary eye on the obvious ringleader. Eye contact is not always a good idea and Clyde agreed with that. He did not approve of Nell's being out of the truck and he definitely did not approve of her making eye contact with him. He charged.

Nell charged too, except that, being of sound mind and body and wishing to keep that relationship intact, she charged backward. The scene must have looked like a movie with the film strip reversed.

Nell got to the truck first and Clyde's 90 pounds or so closed the door firmly. Nell radioed for backup.

It only took me a few minutes to get to the scene. Nell was once again out of the van but maintaining a safe distance from the two dogs and a close relationship to the left-open door of the van. The dogs now seemed to be fairly calm.

I stepped out of my van empty-handed and met with Nell on the sidewalk for a conference since radio transmissions are necessarily brief and consist mainly of simple information given in Ten Code.

I wasn't being Mister Macho when I stepped out of the van empty-handed. I just didn't have the full picture yet.

In retrospect, and for future reference, I should have anticipated a need for protection as Nell filled me in with the missing details.

Every dog capture is different. Also, every officer is an individual who has, through experience, determined what methods work best for him. I have, for example, found that many times an aggressive dog can be quieted and handled with a soft approach. This makes it easier on both the dog and the officer.

On the other hand, there are times when the officer is just plain stupid. This was one of those times for, in spite of Nell's briefing and admonitions, I chose the wrong approach.

For starters, I did not know that the big guy's name was Clyde and names were not up at the top of my concerns at that moment. I might have called him by name if I had known.

What I did know was that the dog was big and I could see that he was most likely a wolf-hybrid, probably crossed with a Malamute. Nell's briefing, had I listened more attentively, would have told me in no uncertain terms that he had already exhibited hostile signs and that he was not an average docile dog.

I started a slow approach toward the pair, concentrating my attention on the big boy. He didn't fool around any. He charged immediately, and even if I had known his name, I would not have thought to use it in the crisis.

He seemed to go from dead stop to Mach One in an instant. With ears laid back and hackles raised, he hurled his body across the intervening space at a prodigious rate of speed. I was instantly not so stupid and immediately realized that I was in trouble. Clyde may have topped out at about 90 pounds, but hurling toward me like a hairy juggernaut, he looked more like 200 pounds. I had encountered wolf-dogs before but never from this disadvantage point. It was inspirational, to say the least.

I yelled for Nell to hand me her baton and I reached behind my back to grab it. I dared not divert my eyes from what was coming toward me, even had I wanted to. My right hand flailed frantically behind my back and Nell frantically attempted to hit my outstretched hand with the baton. We never got it together.

Meanwhile, Clyde was boring down for the kill. I knew that this dog was about ready to go airborne and that I was not going to get my hands on a weapon in time to do any good. Time slowed and both the dog and I moved in half-time. I knew that somehow I must stop this half dog, half monster before he leaped. So little time left.

I dropped down into a half-crouch, that ancient defensive posture, and lowered my voice a couple of octaves, reaching for my best military resonance. I commanded the dog to halt. It came out of my constricted throat more like a barely audible squeak. But somehow, that shrill utterance sank into the dog's hot brain and he recognized the command and obeyed it. He skidded to a stop mere inches from my shaking knees and drew a line in the sand. He stood his ground there, snarling and snapping at me while drooling all over my legs.

Nell came to my assistance again, this time with the appropriate equipment and we soon had Clyde and his companion in tow.

After a few days and a lot of impound and fine fees, Clyde was allowed to return to his newly constructed, escape-proof kennel, at home.

I kept track of him after that, for a couple of years in fact, and got to know him a bit better. He sired a litter of shepherd-wolf pups before he was neutered and was actually a rather nice guy, all in all.

But he was wolf. And he was never allowed to run loose again.

JEKYLL AND HYDE

It was just a routine day at Animal Control. In came a phone call from a lady who said she had lost her cat.

NORMALLY we do not take a complete missing report on cats on the first day a feline is reported missing as many come home after a night out on the town. Not compiling full reports immediately helps keep the lost and found register at a manageable level.

But this time the cat had been missing for three or four days so I proceeded to record a complete report. Name: Fuzzy; address, phone number, description and so forth. It turned out to be a good decision.

A few days later the same lady called back. Since I had taken the original call, she asked for me. She started out by telling me that she had found Fuzzy.

"Great!" I said.

"Not so," she retorted. "They won't give him back to me," to which I naturally inquired as to who 'they' were. "The people who have my cat," she answered. With such sparkling repartee, small wonder we ever solve anything, but eventually I managed to piece together the story.

She explained that she had been walking the neighborhood looking for her pet when she suddenly spied a feline in a window that looked a lot like hers. She crossed the yard and went to the window for a closer look and golly gee, it *WAS* her cat all right. It even recognized her and began to pace back and forth on the window sill, tail up in happy salute and body plastered against the glass as cats are prone to do when pleased.

She went to the door and knocked. She explained to the lady of the house all about the cat being missing and how nice it was that she had found it and she was now ready to take it home.

The lady's response: No way! Go away! Get lost and stay that way! So entered Animal Control.

I started by doing a more intensive interview with the lady who had lost the cat in the first place. Where did she get the animal? How long had she had it? Who was her veterinarian? Did she have medical records, photographs, so forth and so on.

It soon became obvious, in view of the evidence she was able to present, that she did indeed own the cat, if, that is, what she had seen at the other house was in fact her pet. I borrowed some of the better pictures of Fuzzy that she had taken over the years and proceeded to the other house to confront Lady No. Two. If the photos match, that's it.

Said lady was most cooperative but equally adamant that Lady No. One was just trying to get her hands on a nice cat that did not belong to her. After all, who did she think she was, coming to her door and demanding the cat. "I have my rights!" was her stubborn argument, and on and on.

I let her run down and get the anger out of her system. I have learned over time that it is useless to try to reason with someone caught up in the flames of righteous indignation, especially when it concerns a pet.

When she had cooled to less than the molten point of lead, I began again, asking her the same routine questions. I got much the same answers and she was equally compelling in her beliefs that the cat was hers. She also had evidence much the same as I had already seen from Lady No. One.

Two proofs, but was there just one cat? It was time to take a look for myself. I had to convince Lady No. Two that I was not going to grab Fuzzy and run. Finally, she went to the back of the house and came forth with the cat.

I began to doubt my senses. It was indeed a match.

Both ladies had the same data and both had equally defini-
tive proof. This could not be, I reasoned. They could not both be
the rightful owners. Could they?

It was time to beat a retreat and marshal my resources, if
indeed I had any. I mumbled something inane about reviewing the
evidence and departed.

Back at the office, I went over my notes and the testimony of
the two alleged owners. It just did not add up. And then it hit me.
It did add up.

As improbable as it was, to the point of absurdity, they did
indeed both own the same cat. The substantiation was clear, once
I got past the notion that it could not happen. You see, both
women agreed about one thing. They each claimed to own the
same cat. I had merely overlooked the obvious. The little stinker
had been living a dual life!

Once the answer was clear, I knew that I had my work cut
out for me. Convincing them was not going to be easy. But the
answer was there. The cat spent his days at one house, playing
with the kids and being pampered by the stay-at-home mom.
Then, in the evening when he was let out, he went to his other
home. So Lady No. One thought he was just doing his nighttime
cat thing while he was in reality wending his way over to Lady
No. Two who was now home from work and looking forward to
spoiling her little darling.

It was time for a three-way conference. I arranged a meeting,
although both were reluctant to participate. When I completed
presenting my case, they began to compare notes and stories
about Fuzzy—his attitudes, likes and dislikes, behavioral patterns
and food preferences.

Even though they had both been reluctant to accept my
conclusions in the beginning, they were soon forced to look at the
issue head-on. They both owned the same cat. The sly guy was
living two lives, one by day, one by night.

The solution? Why fight it? Let him do what he does so well—
occupy both homes. And so they did. The last I heard, it is all still
working just fine, especially for the cat.

"You think it's easy being a cat??"

SHAFTED

*The telephone rang about 9:30 that evening just
as I was savoring an early bedtime so I felt lucky
that whoever was calling was doing it early. The
voice I recognized immediately banished that
notion and simultaneously raised a new one, as
yet unclear.*

IT WAS NELL, my fellow officer. I knew her as well qualified and
self-reliant. So, I also knew then that we had a problem of some
magnitude or she wouldn't have called me at home. It was her
week to cover the duty phone and she obviously had encountered
an emergency.

She soon filled me in. We had a dog down a mine shaft.
Nevada is called the 'Silver State' for good reason. Millions of
dollars were taken out of her soil in the form of gold and silver,
much of which helped finance the Civil War.

The bulk of the ore was extracted by big companies employ-
ing hundreds of miners, tons of equipment and thousands of
man-hours in support operations.

Those major mining operators had fairly well filled in and
sealed off their properties so there were no longer wide open
shafts. However, a number of smaller private mines had been
dug. Some yielded enough to make them profitable while others
proved to be worthless. In either event, those smaller mines were
simply abandoned, uncapped, when they were no longer of value.

The miners and prospectors had merely walked away,
without a backward glance, in search of newer, richer finds. Many
years later there are thus still mines that have never been filled in

or sealed and this mine was one of them. It was located in the sandy range east of Carson City. A number of almost-roads crisscrossed the area and offered hiking opportunities as well as a good chance to get stuck in the deep sand.

Several couples, it seemed, decided that one of these trails looked like a good spot to hike away from humanity and took off in pursuit of tranquility. One of them took their dog along.

Three quarters of the way up one of the taller slopes they spotted what looked like a hole in the hillside and went up to explore. Yep, it was a horizontal mine shaft.

The dog took off first and heedless of their calls, kept on going. They followed it into the shaft as far as they could and called for the dog as they went, but the dog either would not, or perhaps could not return.

Have you ever entered a cave or tunnel? The darkness closes in on you rather rapidly as you proceed in farther. Soon the darkness is overwhelming and without flashlights you had better stop. That's how people disappear.

Well, just as they reached the point where they realized they had to stop, they spotted a vertical shaft which spanned the width of the tunnel floor and there was no way to go but down. Or build a bridge.

And since there was no bridge, it was clear that the dog had gone down. On hands and knees at the edge of the shaft they peered down and called. Visually, the effort was a waste. It was too dark to see anything and no way to determine where the bottom might be. Ten feet? Or a thousand?

Happily, they heard a welcome bark from below but they could not tell for certain how far down was 'down.' They decided that they needed to go for help.

Nell was on duty and she got the call. When I asked her what time this all started, she told me about 6:00 p.m. But hey, it's 9:30 now. Where has everybody been meanwhile?

Well, Nell tried and almost got to the site but the sandy soil trapped her. The van slid off the road and she had to be towed out. But she did get a chance to look over the mine and the situation but that was all she could get done before dark.

She had a flashlight with her but the shaft just seemed to eat up the light. She didn't get a gleam back from the dog's eyes and that should have happened if the dog had been in line with the light beam.

That could mean that the shaft was a really deep one but that didn't seem likely since the dog could be heard rather clearly. The other explanation was that perhaps another shaft branched off from the first one.

Nell had stopped only long enough to call the Fire Department and arrange to pick up some rope and climbing gear in the morning. So there was nothing further that could be done that night. We opted to wait for dawn and try again.

We got an early start and first light found us nearly at the top of the hill bouncing around in a borrowed four-wheel drive pickup truck. I do mean bouncing.

And thank God for big knobby tires. We did a lot of slipping and sliding but kept on going. I was busy wondering if my derriere would break before I might be pitched headlong out of the back of the truck, together with the equipment. As luck would have it, neither happened and we were soon near the top of the ridge and parked near the opening of the shaft. Faintly but distinctly we could hear a frenzied barking from the bowels of the mine shaft. We still had a very active dog somewhere down there.

I went ahead and checked out the mine while Nell and the others got the gear ready. I also tried the flashlight bit to find out how deep the shaft was but it continued to eat the light without revealing much.

I'm not particularly fainthearted but neither am I light-headed. I really wanted to find out where the bottom was before I started down. We already had a dog stuck down there and I didn't want to add to the list, especially with me. It was obvious that shining the light down there was not going to provide an answer. So we fed the rope down, on the theory that when it hit bottom its length would equal the shaft's depth. The only problem was that we couldn't feel when the rope hit bottom. So we just threw rocks down and guessed at the depth by the sound of the rocks hitting bottom. Conclusion: It couldn't be much over forty feet or so.

Nell had borrowed a lot of gear from the Fire Department including a body harness of some sort and rappelling clips and climber's rope. But since I had never used any of that gear, I figured it would be safer for me to just do it the good old-fashioned way.

It really wasn't too hard going down, sort of like walking down a wall. I just wondered how it would be going up. And with a dog.

Pretty soon the bottom came up to meet me and I could hear the dog off somewhere to my left. But even after I called him by name he did not respond to me so I knew that something was stopping him. He was sure eager enough. He just couldn't make it.

I knew that miners often followed veins of gold as they twisted through the earth so I figured that must have been the case here. If they lost a vein, they drilled a new shaft or started a new tunnel until they either figured it was gone or they picked it up again. That explained why that mine shaft was originally horizontal and then went vertical. That's where the vein went. Now the vein went somewhere else. But where?

I flashed the light in front of me and started a slow circle, looking for another horizontal shaft. About half way around I found one but kept going until the circle was completed, just to make sure there was only one.

Then I went back around until it showed up again. I had gone only a few feet forward when it became clear that this was the way to the dog. His bark was directly to the front and after a few more feet, I found him.

At my feet the shaft ended in a large bowl-like depression, perhaps eight feet deep and a dozen feet around. There the vein had played out and the shaft was abandoned. And there the pooch had played out also, but was not abandoned. He had tried to get out but the sides of the bowl were too steep. Claw marks showed the extent of his efforts.

The rest of it was easy. I still had plenty of rope securely anchored at the top and so I pitched a little of it into the bowl and slid down on it. I said 'hello' to the little spaniel and got him calmed down a bit. You might know it would be a spaniel. God never made a runnier dog, except maybe a Siberian.

I picked him up and pitched him toward the top of the depression and he commenced clawing himself up. A little boost in the butt was all it took to get him over the lip. I joined him there and we were both soon at the bottom of the main vertical shaft where anxious faces peered down at us.

It was a complicated pleasure trying to get the excited dog tied up in the harness so he wouldn't fall out on the way up. The dark didn't help much because even with the lights from above, it was still pretty dim down below.

I, on the other hand, didn't have enough hands to hold a light and easily tie up a squirmer. Anyway, I finally got him secure enough for the topside guys to hoist him up. I figured I could more or less catch him if he slipped out of the harness. He didn't and was soon on top.

Everybody whooped and hollered and in general, forgot all about me. The dog was A-OK and had no broken bones. He probably had glanced half way across the shaft and bounced off the wall repeatedly on his descent, thus breaking his fall. I listened to the topside hubbub and figured they would all wake up the next morning and suddenly remember that they had left me down in the old mine.

Well, with the reunion finally over, they tossed the rope back down to me and up I went. All in all, it was a pretty good morning's work.

I didn't mention it at the time since everyone was in such a jubilant mood, but at the bowl I had found another dog, one not so fortunate. So little remained of him that I did not attempt to remove him from his final resting place.

DOWN THE WELL

It must have been a domino effect. First one board broke and then the next board tipped up on edge and fell into the pit. One or two more shattered and followed the others into the hole. The rider dismounted as the horse went crashing down into the well after the boards which had formerly covered the hole.

IT WAS A MIRACLE that the horse was not pierced by one of the upright steel pipes protruding from the wellhead. He was, however, securely wedged between them and the concrete walls of the pit. And he was heavy.

The calls went out for rescue assistance and one of them came to us because our agency has the word 'animal' in its title and I inherited the assignment. I was probably one of the least qualified people relative to horses that they could have called on for such help.

I do, however, have one advantage that the others lack. I'm stupid enough to go down into the pit with the horse. One other dummy went down with me. I wish I could remember his name so that he could share the Stupid Trick of the Year award but I guess I'll have to bask in that limelight alone.

By the time I arrived on the scene, somebody had thoughtfully procured a backhoe. For the uninitiated, that is an excavation monster on the end of a big stick. It is a huge piece of equipment with lifting capacity and, while it was not designed specifically for lifting horses, it was just what the doctor ordered to solve our dilemma.

Someone had also contributed a pair of thickly woven nylon web slings with lifting rings on either end. The idea was to pass the belts under a heavy object that is to be lifted and to hook the rings onto a hoisting device such as the backhoe that was standing by. It was a good theory.

The slick and tricky part of that process was getting the slings under the tightly squeezed horse. That method was designed for lifting inanimate objects such as pianos or underground fuel tanks, but not horses and especially not horses in wells, and most especially not accompanied by me.

Now horses are neat and I like them a lot. Well, some of them. But I like them best when there is a fence between us. They do trouble me. They are so big. And they're prone to panic, blindly creating crises where none existed before. Supposedly introduced to our shores by the Spanish, I've often wondered how they managed to contain them aboard ship without blundering topside and overboard.

Perhaps my lack of affinity for horses stems from infrequent contact with the beasts. Like there was this one time, for example, when I had to arrest a horse whose owner had enjoyed himself so much at a local beverage shop that he forgot to take the horse home with him at closing time.

It just happened that there was a corral nearby that wasn't being used and I elected to escort the horse there rather than going through the tedious process of containing it, traveling to the Shelter to obtain a horse trailer, loading the animal, transporting and booking it at the center. It is our operational policy to maintain an animal under such circumstances in quarters other than the Shelter if there are available such amenities as the corral in question.

It was at one end of a rough dirt road not far removed from the beverage emporium and I started out leading the horse down the road. The beast had other ideas.

It was quite dark outside and apparently he could see better than I for he bumped and dumped me unceremoniously into the gutter. While I lay prone and defenseless on the ground, he celebrated his triumph by performing a horse version of the Mexican Hat Dance around my head and ears. Fortunately, I came away without hoof prints but with a mouthful of dirt. The episode did little to engender my equine love. But back to the case at hand.

Water wells have been a part of our culture for centuries. We think of them most often as a modestly sized round hole in the ground with a circular brick wall lining the hole and a little roof over the top. Just under the roof is a winch with a rope wrapped around it and a bucket on the end of it.

The more modern version has an electric pump and a bunch of pipes and other confusing equipment. The top of the well is covered over flush with the ground and the whole thing is called a wellhead. Sometimes there is a small structure over the top of the well and sometimes the hole is capped under the surface and then filled up level with dirt and grass so that it is hidden.

This particular well had just been planked over at ground level. It was about ten feet square and at least that deep also. It had been covered with thick planks set flush to the ground on the edge of a concrete wall that lined the pit. It was more than strong enough to walk on and had on many occasions been driven over by cars.

However, it was beginning to show its age and Dad had issued instructions to one and all to avoid traversing it. Period. No cars, no walking, and yes, no horses. That's when a member of the family who shall remain anonymous rode her horse over the pit. So two of us half-wits found ourselves down in the pit to rescue the horse.

Why is it that animals in distress never want to be rescued? They always fight the issue, or at least so it seems. They strive mightily to avoid whatever is being done to help them. And that horse took lessons from other critters in similar circumstances. He utterly failed to cooperate. He twisted, he turned, he bucked as best he could under the circumstances. He nipped, which he could do quite well. We were both battered and bruised but not dead when we finally got the pair of slings under his belly and the hooks secured to the bucket of the backhoe. Finally, up and out went the horse.

Oddly enough, everybody clapped for the rescued animal and ignored us dimwits still in the hole. We did for ourselves what needed to be done. We laboriously climbed out unassisted.

After it was all over, the veterinarian who had been called earlier finally arrived. Shrugging off our tattered egos as well as battered features, he said "Good job, but why didn't you just hook him by the tail and lift him out?" I would think that process would result in rescuing just a handful of hair while the rest of the horse remained in the pit. Not so, claimed the vet in question. He said it was possible to lift the full weight of a horse by the tail which can take the strain without pain or damage to the horse.

Further questioning his statement, a check with other vets in the area countered that opinion.

"I wouldn't want to be below the horse," was their collective reaction. Was the first vet pulling our leg?

I just hope that I won't ever again have the chance to prove the theory, one way or the other.

THOR

*I first met Thor when I picked him up running
loose on the streets. He and I hit it off immediately. Buds.*

FOR ONE THING, Thor was my kind of dog, the one, the only,
German Shepherd. As a breed I consider this dog as being in a
class by itself. And Thor was, at least in my opinion, entitled to a
position at the head of the class.

He deserved his name, Thor being the Norse god of thunder,
weather, war and other categories. He was all German Shepherd
and possessed all of the visual characteristics that made the breed
so attractive. He was also big, meaning impressive. He was a good
watchdog, alert and responsive and would obviously brook no
nonsense should anybody have that in mind.

Unclaimed in the shelter, he was adopted by a young lady
who was employed by the Forest Service.

Whenever I found myself in his neighborhood with a minute
or two to spare, I stopped by and we visited a bit. His owner had
cut a diamond-shaped aperture in the otherwise solid gate so
Thor could stick his head out and have a look around. He would
first check me out to see if I had brought him a treat. And afterward, with or without a treat, he put his great head out for a good
ear rub.

Thor had gotten out a time or two and strolled through
the neighborhood, just like other dogs do occasionally. Once he
was out for a walk and encountered an acquaintance of mine
who called me to see if I could trace the owner. At that time
said caller also told me he would dearly love to keep Thor.

However, since I recognized the dog and knew his owner, that was not an option.

Another time Thor had a head-on collision with a car. The contest ended in a draw. The car stopped dead in its tracks and Thor went down for an eight count. Unconscious but otherwise unharmed, he recovered.

It was some time later that Thor's owner called me and literally shocked me out of my socks. She expressed an interest in finding a new home for Thor. It was more than an interest actually. It was an intent.

Through Thor we had become acquainted and she felt certain that I could find a new home for him. She wished for nothing but the best for her dog but she felt that she and Thor should part company. This I could not understand and I told her so.

The explanation for her astounding attitude was lengthy but essentially, she felt that she and Thor had not been able to bond, achieve that special feeling, that joining of master and pet that develops a rapport. She said that it was lacking between them and that in spite of all the good times they had together, she felt that the dog had not related to her in that special way.

Now, I am not a dog psychologist but I have lived long enough to acquire some understanding of both people and dogs. Despite her protestations to the contrary, her constant companionship with Thor was to be envied. Her rationale I could not accept. There simply had to be more to this than met the eye.

I'll have to admit that my prejudice or bias in favor of German Shepherds encouraged me to look into the matter in greater depth than I would have if it had been, perhaps, a Lhasa Apso. With this bias in place, I could not perceive the Shep's being at fault. So I reasoned, it must be the owner who is off-base.

On closer scrutiny, it seems that Thor was not the first German Shepherd in this young lady's life. Her previous dog had also been such a Shep. And she was, at that time, employed by the Forest Service and was on fire watch duty. For days at a time, her only companion was her dog. Always there. Ever faithful. It was axiomatic that a strong relationship should develop between them. Then came the shock of her faithful companion's demise.

So after considering all that I knew about Thor's personality, I felt that I had to inject myself into the problem and find a solution as well. The question was, could I convince her of what I felt to be the truth? Who was it who said, "The fault lies not in our stars but in ourselves?" Anyway, that was my contention and I had to convince her that the fault, the lack of bond, did not come from Thor, but rather resided in herself. Meanwhile I had contacted the gent to whom I had spoken previously and he was ready to take Thor in a second if my plans didn't work.

So the time was ripe for a heart-to-heart with Thor's owner. I told her of my feelings and of where I thought the real problem lay. I felt that she, quite inadvertently and without conscious intent, was comparing Thor to her previous dog and that poor Thor was coming up short through no fault of his own. It was unreasonable to expect Thor, or any other dog, to measure up to the old memory. It was time now to let Thor be his own man, so to speak. It was necessary for her to love and to cherish Thor for what he was, for himself alone, for his own unique self. There was no real lack but just a perception of lack. If the perception were changed, then the sense of lack would disappear. Thor, I felt, was too valuable to be wasted on a misconception.

I asked only that she think it over and if she decided that Thor must go, and knowing that a good home was waiting in the wings, I would arrange the switch.

Three days later a bottle of champagne was delivered to the Kennel office, along with a thank-you note. My amateur attempt at Psychology 101 had worked! A bond had been recognized and Thor was, for the first time, truly home.

"Has anyone ever told you that
you have funny, fat, furry front feet?"

A LAMENT TO STELLA

It was mid-July. About two hours before sunset I began the steep climb toward the top of the range of hills which run along the southeast side of the Nevada State Prison. Most of the locals refer to those crests as Prison Hill for obvious reason.

THE HILL IS ABOUT forty-five minutes high when ascended at a brisk heart-accelerating pace. I don't know its altitude but the view from the top is exhilarating. At sundown, the city lies below like a twinkling jewel. Off to the east is a snakelike row of trees which mark the course of the Carson River. It is a superb refuge in which to commune because of its solitary ambiance.

But it was there, on the crest of Prison Hill, that I wept for my Stella. It was she who had taken so many hikes with me up there. Stella, the Sheltie, was one of the most precious of God's creatures. Frightened by an exploding firecracker on the Fourth of July, Stella had panicked. She was struck and killed by an automobile.

All who knew her came to love her. She, like many of her kind, had a mission here: to show us how to give unconditional love. She did it well and we who knew her will miss her. I therefore dedicate this reverie to her memory and to the memory of all those others who, like her, brought light into our darker moments.

Stella had only been under our roof for a few days when she ate the car. I like to think that it was more an act of panic than of appetite, otherwise we had indeed adopted a fearsome monster. Glenna named her because she said if you looked closely into her eyes, you could see tiny little lines of light radiating out from her pupils like stars twinkling. I stretched my imagination to the max but I just couldn't see the star radiations, but what do I know? The proper course of action was to surrender gracefully and concede that Stella was indeed the ideal name for a dog that resembled Lassie.

Stella came to us as the result of a late evening call relayed to our home phone from the Sheriff's Office. I was the standby officer on duty that night.

The call came from the manager of a local motel who had discovered that one of his tenants was harboring an unauthorized canine in his room. The manager requested a pick-up. The guest insisted he just found the dog out at the edge of town.

I personally suspected that she really belonged to the motel guest and that he just got caught with her in his room. He had not paid the required pet deposit and I suspected in addition that he was down on his luck and had no choice but to give her up.

Normally dogs such as Stella are booked into the pound and kept there for a period of time before they are made available to the public for adoption in the event an owner does not come forward to claim them. The fact that no one ever came forward to rescue Stella lends credibility to my theory.

It was pretty late at night when I picked her up and got all the stories collected and so, against the rules, I took her home with me. After all, we do have a provision that allows a finder to retain custody of a found dog pending owner identification. It calls for appropriate ID of both the finder and the critter as well as other information needed to allow an owner to find and reclaim a lost pet.

The finder will eventually gain legal title to the animal by reason of the continued possession of it, coupled with the failure of any otherwise lawful owner to come forward. I took advantage of this rule quite legally and appropriately and after a couple of days, Stella had wiggled in close enough to both of us that we began to consider keeping her. She clinched it herself one night when Glenna was feeling low.

"Stella!" she called and the dog responded and went bouncing into the bedroom but didn't move especially close. "Oboy," Glenna continued. "That's all I need, a dog that doesn't show any affection just when I really need it!"

Aha! Stella heard that and figured out real quick that her home was not yet in the bag. She immediately buried her long Lassie nose in Glenna's arms and let out the most soulful groan anybody ever heard. That cinched it. Stella stayed.

We were still getting accustomed to her ways and had no idea of her propensity to eat cars from the inside out. I learned about that one the hard way. I had parked at the supermarket, not to shop, but to inspect some jangling I heard coming from the trunk. Getting out, I gave Stella a firm "No!" when she indicated she wanted to follow me. The car windows were open so she had no reason to emerge.

It was then I discovered a friend parked just a few cars away and so we had a yak session while I pursued the noisy contents of the trunk. I, of course, forgot about Stella in the interim. When I finished the chatting and trunk inspection and reclaimed my seat inside the car, I couldn't believe my eyes. Stella apparently had been quietly very busy. The backrest showed signs of her efforts as she left claw-dents in the upholstery. I should have gotten the message then.

Sometimes I offer suggestions about dogs and training and it is often good advice. Maybe I should listen to myself. I certainly missed the boat that time.

A couple of weeks later we decided to take a day trip and took Stella along. The destination was only a two-hour drive. Along the route the highway paralleled the Walker River for a couple of miles. There were several really good spots for dog romping. We had a great time learning more about our new dog and her relationship to flowing water. We stayed dry. She stayed wet. Don't you just love the swell smell of a newly wet dog? Ranks right up there with cow pastures, doesn't it?

Eventually we played ourselves out and headed toward the end of the trail. That's when we spotted a big burger stand. Glenna went in to get our food while I again busied myself checking on the back tire that had picked up a small rock somewhere on the highway and was making a disturbing clatter as we traveled. Again, with car windows wide open, I gave Stella the "No" command when she offered to join me. I paid no further attention to her until Glenna arrived with our food. As it turned out, Stella had ideas of her own about being left alone, even briefly. That's when I lost it, hopping and screaming all at once, not unlike a whirling dervish in stereo. The car's interior looked like a target for a terrorist team in training. The driver's seat was shredded. The headliner hung in streamers like crepe paper after the prom. One of the door's side panels had been pried loose from its retaining clips until only the doorknob held it in place.

The car was a wreck. Repairable, yes, but a casualty. Certainly if it had been a place instead of a thing it could have qualified for disaster relief.

Stella simply looked up at me and wagged her tail excitedly, so pleased with herself.

But for all of her destructive inclinations, Stella was a superb art critic. Local historians like to relate, *ad nauseam*, that Carson City was named, not after Johnny of Tonight Show fame, or after the river that almost flows through the city. During most years, although usually somewhat shy in volume, the Carson River meanders more or less *around* the town.

Anyway, it was that other guy that Nevada's capital, and the river, were named for—the Indian guide, frontier scout and all-around explorer, Kit Carson. He just didn't stick around long enough to accept the honor.

In commemoration of Kit's historical significance, the City Fathers, also known as the Board of Supervisors, decided to erect some endurable art and forthwith commissioned a statue to be created in memory of Scout Kit Carson and that it be lodged in a place of honor in the town square. But since the city had no town square, they decided to petition the State for permission to place the statue, when created, on the grounds of the State Legislature complex.

The State did permit such usage and thereupon the Board commissioned an artist to do the deed.

I'm sure it wasn't all that easy. I mean, they couldn't just pick someone at random to do the job. Civic projects are simply not done that way.

They probably created a committee to do the actual choosing from a list of prospective prequalified candidates.

The committee itself no doubt had to be composed of an odd number of persons, say like five, so that one of them could cast a tie-breaking vote if necessary.

I'm sure the committee elected to have an artist or at least an art critic on the commission. Certainly a businessman or businesswoman would be needed so as to be politically correct, plus a representative of the government and maybe a person of the cloth. A cleric could assure that there would be no nudes or immodesties please. Oh yes, at least one lawyer would be needed to keep things legal and above board and avoid being sued.

Eventually and finally, the die was cast and an artist was chosen. They picked a sculptor by name of Buckeye Blake. Now that's enough right there to make a taxpayer suspicious. After all, what kind of real artist would be named after a nut? It is bad enough to have a beautiful state like Ohio smeared with the nut name, Buckeye State! A buckeye is a nice enough nut as nuts go but hardly worthy of having states and people named after it. So be it. Buckeye got the job. But the old adage that you can't judge a book by its cover or an artist by his name is still valid.

About then I had occasion to arrest a horse, a beautiful all-white stallion. Maybe 'arrest' is incorrect. It occurred during a notable event held annually in Carson City called, understandably, the Kit Carson Rendezvous. That's when a whole bunch of guys and gals dress up in buckskins and Bowie knives, carry hatchets and black-powder rifles and ride around on horseback or covered wagons and do other western stuff. The local Native Americans sell Indian tacos and the Kiwanis sell hot dogs and beer. It's a grand time, really.

The event takes place mainly in Carson City's Mills Park where the little choo-choo train, which is the park's main attraction, runs its little wheels off carting grown-ups and kids galore around in circles through the area. The people, horses, wagons, donkeys, mules, knives and tomahawks all mill around in the park that weekend and have a wonderful time.

There is, of course, one problem. The park is closed to animals. And horses, donkeys and mules are animals. But since those equine types carry the people and pull the wagons which contain the rendezvous participants, what is the City to do about that?

So comes a solution.

The Park Service, in keeping with the spirit of the occasion and by virtue of authority vested in it by the Board of Supervisors, suspends the restrictions against animals for the duration of the event. Thus, the park is opened to the horses, donkeys, mules and sometimes burros and camp dogs that accompany the buckskin people. Opened, but only *during the event*. Not before, not after, but only during.

But it seems there was one personification of mountain man who wanted to show off his magnificent stallion without the benefit of the competition offered by the rest of the wagon trains' entourage the day before opening of the big event. So he was a bit early in the park, one day early, to be exact. He trotted and cavorted with his steed through the park to the open admiration of the park habitues. Rumor had it that he may have imbibed a bit too freely of the adult style beverages that are always abundantly present at these affairs.

The Park Service was dismayed at this open and flagrant abuse of its authority and enlisted the support of the Sheriff's office to assist in removing the mounted menace from the premises. Not wishing to create any disharmony during the days of Kit Carson, they politely but firmly removed rider and horse from the park. Twice. On the third time around they decided that a bit more firmness was in order.

Apparently the stallion objected to this show of authority on the part of the officers who were attempting to effect an arrest. He threw his owner-rider off his back. This development made apprehension of the human offender somewhat easier but created a more difficult problem with regard to the stallion which had a mind of its own and promptly headed for the nearest casino.

During the ensuing pursuit on and off the parking area adjacent the casino, a black and white patrol car was somewhat damaged as said stallion was clipping along at a goodly pace on the sidewalk, fast approaching a traffic signal on the corner. One of the officers decided that the horse would most likely not be familiar with the concept of traffic control and would ignore the red light. So, in a well-intentioned move, he interposed his vehicle between the horse and the intersection. Only one slight miscalculation marred the efficacy of this plan. The horse was shod. Stopping a half ton of frisky horseflesh is not an easy task, especially when it is wearing steel shoes and is running on smooth concrete instead of cushiony sod.

It happened that the stallion's brakes did not work too well and he was only slightly cut. The patrol car was somewhat dented and one side window sort of disappeared into fragments. However, the goal was accomplished in the end and the horse was apprehended.

It was at this point that I was called in from my off-duty stint as a representative of Animal Control. It was my chore to come and get the horse. The rider was going to go to the drunk tank to sober up and contemplate the error of his ways. In the meantime something had to be done with the horse.

Normally I do not haul a horse trailer around with me on my day off and this day was no exception. I do, however, live not far from the scene of the incident where the horse was being held. So, I simply picked up his reins and led him home, my home that is. Once there, I popped my head inside the door and told my unsuspecting wife to please look after the horse until I returned with a trailer to retrieve him.

Glenna, bless her understanding heart, never batted an eye at this strange request. Perhaps she did not at first believe it, that is, until she finally realized that the ruckus outside really was a horse tied to the front porch.

Stella, on the other hand, took instant umbrage at this sacrilegious use of her front yard. Stella's limited prior acquaintance with stallions had always been at a respectful distance and they had always been where they belonged: in a pasture and behind a fence. This one was in *her* yard. Such was simply not to be borne with equanimity and she did not so bear it. She was, in a word, frantic.

Eventually the night passed and so did the horse in the front yard and Stella was mollified. Apparently though, she did not forget it.

Meanwhile, Glenna, Stella and I chose to stroll the Legislative complex. There, Stella, in one simple act, vindicated the judgment of the Committee, the Commissioners and most of all, the superb talents and abilities of one Buckeye Blake who had cast in bronze the commemorative statute of Kit Carson astride a mighty steed in the middle of the legislature's lawn. At the sight of Kit Carson, frontier scout extraordinaire, astride the rearing stallion with the wild eyes and bared teeth, Stella went bonkers. Buckeye had outdone himself. That is one lifelike horse, one so good in fact that, even without horse scent, it fooled Stella, who still resented any equine presence. A smart dog, that one. I still miss her.

"Your dog ate my lecture notes..."

SILVER LINING

*Joe Fuller is in the hospital tonight. He was
admitted after he went to the emergency room for
treatment. His best friend, Shenandoah, is having
a late night snack at my place.*

SHENANDOAH! It has a nice ring to it. Sorta reminiscent of
something out of a John Wayne movie. Anyway, it's the name of a
nice young lady with which I have the privilege of spending an
unusual evening.

She makes me wonder what Joe is doing, and thinking, in
the hospital tonight. It is about nine o'clock now and I imagine
the nurses are making their final rounds, dispensing sleeping
pills or pain potions and perhaps a glass of juice. It's time to
make the patients as comfortable as possible for the approaching
night's fitful sleep.

Shenandoah is in the corner over by the front door. She
seems to be watching my wife watching TV, not particularly interested in sitcoms, I'd guess.

In the process I'm beginning to see the green monster,
jealousy, raising its ugly head. Stella, my beloved Sheltie, has cast
several meaningful glances in Shenandoah's direction and then at
me, as if to connect the look to me as well. But it's all okay and
Joe would be pleased if he knew. Maybe tomorrow I'll call his
room and tell him about this evening.

Shenandoah is Joe's best girl, a husky type Siberian with a
full black and white coat and a proudly curled tail carried high
over the back. She is indeed lovely. More importantly, she has
both manners and charm to match her looks. These are the

reasons Stella, my dog, is jealous. In spite of all that, Stella, being a Lady herself, is making our guest's stay as pleasant as possible, knowing full well she would hear from me if she didn't.

We have a rule at Animal Control. Actually, it is the law under which we operate. It is a procedure we follow whenever there is an incident that will keep a pet's owner or some other responsible person from continuing to provide care for a pet. It is called, appropriately enough, protective custody and it means that we take into custody, or care for a person's animal whenever one of these incidents occurs that will leave the pet in an uncared-for situation.

This happens for a variety of reasons such as sudden illness or accident, mental instability, death, or an arrest. The law says that we will hold these uncared for animals for a period of 'not to exceed ten (10) days.' During that time we try to locate a friend or relative of the incapacitated person so that the pet can be removed from our custody. Sometimes we will hold the pet for the full ten days and at other times the owner or the owner's appointed representative will retrieve the pet before the end of the appointed period.

If all of this fails, the pet will be made available for adoption. We simply cannot continue to hold it longer. Kennel space and the demands for housing are too limited in the first instance and too persistent in the second.

Joe called me today. He said that he would be there, in the hospital, too long. He was more seriously ill than he thought. He had lived in another state before this and he knew no one here. He was not able to find anyone to care for his pet, his friend.

I did not pry but I sensed a proud but lonely man, one who could place greater store in a canine friend than in a human one. I had not met him face to face, but I liked him. I liked his style, and his courage. Yes, courage.

Who was it who said "Hope springs eternal in the human breast?" That includes courage to face the inevitable with dignity and to make the tough choices rather than relying on false hopes. It takes courage to do what the bumper sticker says: "If you love something, let it go." Joe did just that. He asked me to find a place, a loving place, for Shenandoah. I normally would only agree to look for such a haven. But in this instance, I *promised* to find one.

Sometimes I shine. I did on this one for not only did I find a loving home for the beautiful Shenandoah but I found one that was willing to give her back if Joe recovered enough and could take her back. In essence, it was a foster home for a Siberian, no small feat.

Often when walking through a door it is best to close it behind you and never look back. For this reason I had not told Joe about my special arrangement for his special friend. What could I say to him if the arrangement fell through? So I had kept my own counsel on the matter.

Many weeks passed and new events with new faces and places marched through the time line of events. Joe and Shenandoah moved even further away, out of sight, out of mind, but not forgotten. It took only an instant to bring it all back when they once again came into focus.

When Joe called I made small talk with him and did not tell him more than that I'd found a home for his pet. During the conversation he assured me that he was now okay and that he had a new job and all was well with the world except he terribly missed his dog. He just wanted some reassurance that she was doing well in her new home. He also said he really wanted to get another pet even though none could compare to his beloved Shenandoah.

I took Joe's number and told him I would call him back as soon as I touched base with Shenandoah's new owner to confirm how she was doing.

I made the call to see if the original deal was still on. The new owners were so much in love with her they were most reluctant to give her up. But a deal was a deal. And they honored it.

Joe's joy was unsurpassed when I called him back and told him that Shenandoah was not only alive, but well, and coming home to him. It took several minutes to convince him that it was indeed true and that Shenandoah was never really gone, just borrowed.

I missed the actual reunion but I can imagine it well. That image of Joe's thanks will stay with me forever. It's one of the delightful perks of the job. Joe and Shenandoah were a pair of the lucky ones!

And me? Yes, I would have to say I'm lucky too, lucky enough to have fond memories.

"Couldn't we just trade her in on something fun, like a dog or a horse?"

ADIOS, ADIEU

*The entourage moved slowly along the narrow
road led by a very shiny, very long, black limou-
sine. The party was small and consisted of only
three rather aged automobiles following the lead
limo. There was no hearse. None was needed
although it would have been nice to have had one
available.*

THIS WAS OBVIOUSLY not an affluent group of mourners, but
since when is grief measured by the size of the purse strings?
Opinions might also be formed based upon the sparsity of assembled friends of the deceased. One conclusion might be
reached that the deceased was not well known. Or worse, not well
liked. The consensus might also be reached that the deceased's
passing was of minor import and the group was there out of a
sense of duty rather than a sense of loss. Valid impressions?

It is certainly not customary for a uniformed chauffeur of the
leading vehicle in a funeral procession to be an active member of
the party. Thus, the first note of uncertainty was introduced when
he alighted carrying a silver champagne bucket, complete with a
magnum of champagne. Another member of the group disem-
barked carrying a sheath of plastic disposable glasses. Was
this to be a funeral? Or perhaps a wake?

Actually, as it turned out, it was to be a bit of both. The
deceased was, in fact, not only well loved but truly missed. Each
one in the procession obviously felt the loss deeply. The mourners were all family, at least in a manner of speaking. None of them

physically resembled any of the others, excepting that they were all of similar age: young, early twenties.

Other than the liveried chauffeur, they were all dressed rather informally, quite casually, in fact, in jeans and jogging shoes but all neat and clean. It was as though they all wore their best play clothes.

They all seemed quite happy, almost vivacious. A strange attitude? Strange indeed, for if observing closely, it was possible to see a certain forced nonchalance and more than one eye that was not totally dry. A remark here, a laugh there, all of it a strange keynote. It was an act of stoicism.

Those assembled were the friends, the family of Sundance, the Golden One. Shared alike by one and all, this marvelous Golden Retriever was owned by none. It was a collective family around an open grave. As the body of the Golden One was lowered into the waiting earth, solemn toasts of farewell were offered.

Around the circle each human offered respect and love to the departing canine. A shower of glasses followed the toasts until the last of the circle had made a contribution. A light sprinkle of champagne dotted the casket and a full bottle and clean glasses were laid beside it.

This then was the how and why of Sundance, an unofficial greeter on the other side of the veil. It would be he who would perhaps have the happy duty to ease the passage of newcomers and quiet the grief of those who must bear their loss.

At least I think so.

AND THEN THERE WAS BLONDIE. She would have been four and a half years old today. And she would be four and a half years old tomorrow too because for Blondie, time stood still in its relentless march toward the eternal mystery.

None of us knew her biological mother or father. And her human owners stood with hot dry eyes over her open coffin, quietly mourning her passage into that somewhere that dog friends go when they leave this plane.

Blondie had always been a good friend: loyal, trusting, devoted. Hers had been a difficult role but she had assumed it with a happy heart and a never ceasing willingness to please. Just four years and two months ago she had been selected to fill a void in the grieving hearts of her human companions over the loss of Toby.

Today she would be placed next to Toby, her predecessor pet so beloved by the family. Together, side by side, they would lie as though in state, their bodies buried but their spirits romping through that eternal playground I'm sure God has set aside for dogs.

Toby had been one of those rare pets that crawl inside your mind and heart so thoroughly that nothing can dislodge them. Many of us have had that one truly unique, never to be duplicated, dog. It is rare that we are blessed in one lifetime with more than one. Theirs is a special character that is more than human, more than dog. It is love unfettered by petty jealousies or imagined slights. It is love given endlessly, whether or not deserved, which forms a bond of communication between human and animal that is like no other. Such a love was Toby's and death had created a vacuum that was unfillable by another.

Blondie however, being only a dog, did not know this. So as dogs will do, she gave of herself without reservation, and while not quite able to match Toby in all ways, she nevertheless repaired the rent in her masters' hearts. She had earned for herself that honored spot next to the unforgettable Toby.

Even now, reposed in death within the satin lining of her cherrywood coffin, Blondie emanated her warmth of spirit to all. Her unruly neck ruff still refused to lie flat against her sleek form, giving her a royal air much like an Elizabethan queen's ruffled white collar. So as though in slumber, not in death, she seemed to be saying "I will be gone but I will leave you with memories that will enrich your years until we meet again."

She leaves behind her litter mates, a brother and two sisters whose duty it is to continue her legacy of love. It is a destiny that began that day, four years and two months ago when the four of them were given a second chance by the family, for on that day when Toby was given his final faretheewell, Blondie and her littermates were adopted from the pound and now those mates will bear Blondie's standard in her aggrieved absence.

TIMES WERE A BIT DIFFERENT when I was growing up. The family entertainment center of my youth was four straight-backed chairs arranged in a semicircle around a table-top radio on the mantelpiece. A shared bowl of popcorn and sometimes a pot of hot chocolate completed the amenities of the center.

We avidly 'watched' the radio, listening to *The Shadow*, *The Green Hornet* and the spine-tingling *Inner Sanctum*. Our minds created the pictures we saw as our ears transmitted the sounds of radio to our brains. Comic book characters were alive as were our heroes, together with heroine Wonder Woman with her bullet-bouncing bracelets. Frankenstein joined with the werewolf and the mummy to provide the frights of our lives. Television hadn't yet become a commercial venture.

Then there was that other arena that provided another kind of frightful experience for daring youth, namely the huge old cemetery in the middle of town. God did not create much flat land in our town and the cemetery was no exception. All terrain rolled and dipped with scarcely a level place to be found any-where in that arena. Visibility was limited and the unseen could come from anywhere in those surroundings, particularly with a little imagination. It was old, to be sure. It looked old. It felt old, a musty clammy moldy kind of old.

Gravel driveways wound their narrow ways around and through the hills and valleys of it, first curving to the right and then curving to the left but seldom straight.

Giant spreading oaks and spear-shaped pines held them-selves aloof from white-faced birches. Here and there a willow drooped its way toward the ground. Moss draped it all in wispy webs like spiders' traps.

There was marble, interspersed with concrete and black iron and green copper plus crosses of all description. Eerie shapes with inscriptions pretended to celebrate life but instead saluted death's finality. Add a night wind to sway the trees and mold the shadows to unearthly designs, plus wrought iron gates that were long since frozen open on unyielding hinges, inviting all to enter—if they dared.

We dared, venturesome young bucks. We vied with each other's courage to walk slow, to stop, to peer at crypts and mausoleums and shrines, to listen to the crunch of our feet on the stones and the whisper of things felt in the night air. The ultimate act of courage was to go alone to a barren crypt and to stand there, fists tightly clenching the bars and wait. Wait for those inside to become aware of our presence. To face the unseen alone was the challenge. And then, after the quickening, to walk away, slowly. Not one of us ever did all of that successfully. Fear lends wings to the stoutest of hearts.

Many years later, in a more advanced state of age and maturity, I was privileged to participate in the design, development and construction of a far different place for the departed. It was the Sierra Vista Pet Cemetery, adjacent the Carson City Animal Shelter, created to provide a final resting place for pets.

It comprised a simple grassy area with trees and bushes, with planters and a minimum of fences and walkways. It is, we hope, a tranquil place, a place to find peace. We think it has served the community well and what is more, it does not frighten anyone, not even kids.

JUST CALL ME CHICKEN

"Whatever it was that was in my back yard last night was a big sucker," she said. "It done got the dogs all riled up and it's a good thing they were indoors, else I don't know what would have happened. You come and look and you'll see," she concluded.

 **SO WE DID.** She was right on one count. It was big. A fairly large but still young tree grew in the back yard near the storage shed. I suppose its trunk was maybe seven or eight inches thick. One entire side was completely stripped of bark from about head high to within a couple of feet off the ground.

It had been stripped by claws, not teeth, and the claw lines cut deeply into the tree. There was no question about it. She had been visited by a bear during the night and it was probably a good thing that the dogs had been inside, else they might not have survived, for while dogs are pretty good at fending off intruders, they don't fare too well if a bear gets a grip on them.

There are a few bears around the Sierra foothills but mostly you don't see them as they tend to shy away from people, unless hungry. Even hikers rarely see them. Once in a while though, they will come down to browse the garbage cans and the like. If they get too persistent in this type behavior, they have to be trapped and transported to a truly remote area.

There was this one occasion when we had an injured bear. He was found lying off to the side of the road early one morning by a couple of construction guys on their way to work.

The bear was out cold, probably had been hit by a car, and needed some help. So the two Samaritans took a sheet of plywood out of their truck and made a ramp out of it to slide the bear up and into the truck. It was not full-grown yet, bigger than a cub, smaller than an adult. But he was big and fat enough to require two husky men to load it. Anyway, they brought it to us.

By the time we got it, the bear was regaining consciousness and starting to move around a bit, more than we wanted it to. We needed to get it to a veterinarian but we didn't have anything in which to transport it except doggy vans.

So, we gave it a mild shot of tranquilizer and sent him back to a groggy state before loading it into the back of the van. The question foremost in my mind as I climbed into the driver's seat was: Did we give him enough to keep him quiet until I got him to the vet's? How do you know when the dose is enough?

Judge it by comparable advice. They say that a rattlesnake, when coiled, is able to strike and hit a distant object two-thirds of its body length away. So how close can you safely get? It's simple. Just pick up the snake and measure its length from the tip of its snout to the end of its last rattle. Now divide that distance by three and multiply by two. Put the snake back down and don't walk any closer than the distance you just calculated.

So how do you do it with a bear? Again, it's simple. The recommended dosage for our particular tranquilizer is one cc per ten pounds of body weight. So you first pick up the bear and weigh it and then calculate the proper dosage, presuming the bear is nice and friendly.

We did none of the above and measured the dose a little on the light side because of the unknown nature and extent of the bear's injury. While en route to the vet, the bruin began to move. So did I.

It is a mite nerve-wracking to realize that a bear bigger, fatter and heavier than I am is moving around in the back seat. I knew the ties on the stretcher wouldn't hold a bear that doesn't want to be held. And there was no superstructure that separated him from me, he being in a mere dog vehicle. Since I didn't know how serious his injuries were, I also didn't know what his capabilities were.

It all obviously worked out okay. The bear slept restlessly while I drove recklessly, and we both arrived at the animal hospital in pretty much the same shape we started. Like I said, call me chicken, but I had seen what those claws could do to a tree trunk which is considerably tougher than my flesh and I didn't want to be a guinea pig for a further test.

Wild animals are dangerous to handle and any officer or game warden who sets out to capture them has to use extreme caution. The speed and power of a wild animal is almost always underestimated. And all too often, when someone fails to assess the dangers of dealing with such, they pay a tremendous price as even small animals can cause serious damage.

So, the best advice when it comes to handling wild animals is, don't.

"So there I was, hibernating in this
snowdrift when along comes some skier
who mistakes me for a mogul..."

TEDDY

Teddy was his name and terror was his game.
Feline terror, that is. He was my first dog. His
parentage was more or less uncertain but to a
child of nine, his lineage could hardly be a matter
of much concern. I only knew that he was a good
buddy who was always ready for a romp in the
vacant lots behind our house.

ONE OF HIS REALLY NIFTY TRAITS was his ability to lie beside
me, warm and comforting, exuding love and strength while I
quivered in fear listening to *Inner Sanctum* on the radio. Really
scary stuff, that. Only those who profess to being 'not as young as
I used to be' will be able to relate to that. They now call it the good
ole days of radio.

If you were around then you will remember some of those
shows and you'll have to admit that while they would be pretty
mild today, they were plenty spooky then. And Teddy was always
there, offering moral support even though he couldn't understand
that he was doing it. He was just a good friend in a doggy suit,
white with a couple of black spots and one brown one for good
measure, with ears that almost stood up straight.

But he was the cat scourge of the neighborhood, because
back then we had no leash laws and dogs ran free. I always felt
that Teddy wouldn't actually hurt one of those cats because he
never got close enough, but bejabbers how he would chase them!

No cat was secure on the ground when Teddy was on the
loose and every cat within six blocks of our house knew it. When

Teddy took a stroll, the trees suddenly became liberally plastered with hackle-raised cats, or so it seemed to me. Now, as an adult, I would correct that sort of behavior, but back then I admired Teddy's machismo.

There was one cat in particular that Teddy delighted in treeing and he did it so often that I almost began to feel sorry for the cat. And apparently the cat also got tired of feeling sorry for herself and decided to do something about the neighborhood bully.

The cat, Hope, lived in a big two-story house on the corner three or four houses down the street. Hope had a lot of people living with her in that big dwelling. All the kids however were girls, so I didn't have too much to do with them. After all, I was nine and at that age girls were ugh! It wasn't as though they were real people or anything.

Apparently all of the older females had rooms upstairs and those rooms could be reached by an outside stairway, although I never saw anybody use it. But Hope certainly knew it was there.

One day I was coming back from playing with Marvin and Melvin who lived just down the street from us, down the block from the corner house. People today would call them African Americans or maybe Blacks but we just called them friends. Twins they were, but not quite identical so we could, sometimes, tell them apart.

I think that Marvin or Melvin, or both of them together, invented the skate board. Or maybe it was some of their kin. That was 50 years ago or more. I'm sure they never made a dime out of the invention but they did create the board because all of the kids in their extended family had skate boards.

The only difference then and now is that back then the boards had an upright stick at the front of the board and a little 'T' member nailed at the top of the stick, making a sort of scooter. The bottom board was flat and equipped with roller skate wheels front and back. They made them out of scrap lumber and discarded skates. Often, the upright stick would break off and what was left was a skateboard, complete with dog aboard.

Returning from playing at Marvin and Melvin's place one day, I noticed Hope crouched down at the corner of the big two-story house. Following her gaze I spotted Teddy marching down the sidewalk, heading toward me.

Teddy had a way of walking tall when he was on the prowl. Head held high with tail carried erect to match, he high-stepped like a horse on parade. That walk spelled CAT-astrophe for somebody and Hope, peeking around the corner of a geranium bed, recognized it. I swear that you could almost see the light bulb appear above Hope's head as the idea was born.

This was a cat brain at work. Hope apparently knew that Teddy's route, Teddy being a creature of habit, would bring him down the street and around the corner and, Whoopee! Under the staircase landing. Up the stairs went Hope.

I began to get the same light bulb above my head that Hope had gotten as the idea of revenge began to form. I too, began to understand the plan.

I suppose I could have stopped it right then and there but I didn't. Maybe I felt that Teddy was due a comeuppance, which he was, and maybe I didn't really understand the potential for damage. At any rate, I didn't intercept it.

Hope inched her body forward until she was literally perched on the edge of the landing, both front and rear feet in line, balanced like a tightrope walker with four legs. Teddy cock-of-the-walked around the corner and passed directly under the landing. Hope launched.

Time and motion seemed to slow as Hope floated down, down, down toward Teddy, from two stories up. Teddy, for his part, maintained his stately pace but slowed in the same time frame as the approaching cat.

Hope began to paw the empty air, front and back together, a four-wheel-drive cat. Ever more rapidly the paws clawed the air until they no longer appeared to be paws, but wheels, blurred with speed.

Hope struck the unsuspecting dog just above the eyes and seemed to break off the attack immediately. But those four razor-tipped wheel-paws had done the job, all in an instant. Poor Teddy stood like a poleaxed steer with legs spread wide, shaking his head slowly back and forth. He must have had a thousand cuts and practically no hair left at all. It was the quickest trim job I'd ever seen. Hope had almost scalped Teddy.

I had no idea that a cat could do that and would not have allowed it to happen had I even had a clue as to the amount of damage a cat could inflict. But I didn't know and Teddy paid for my ignorance and his arrogance, all at the same time.

Teddy never did chase Hope again after that incident but they did develop the first Cold War, each carrying off a certain bravado whenever chance brought them into semiproximity. I also noticed that thereafter they were each very careful to avoid issuing a challenge that would have to be answered.

Teddy never rescued anyone from a burning building or a drowning or anything like that but he had the stuff of heroes. He just never had the opportunity to prove himself. He once did have the chance to show off his prowess as a watchdog and he did so. Unfortunately, his human counterparts failed to do their part and Teddy lost out on his well-deserved Medal of Honor.

It happened one Christmas season. We never considered ourselves poor. I guess if we didn't think so, we weren't. Granted, certain things were sort of beyond our reach so we just did without them. We didn't dwell on the subject.

For example, my brother and I shared a bike. We worked out a schedule for using it and rarely had a conflict about it. It just usually worked out that Jack used it when he wanted it and I used it when he didn't.

Every joint in that bike had been broken at least once and rewelded. The inner tubes were a series of assorted sizes of hot and cold patches, held together by strips of the original tubes. And the whole thing had been repainted more times than the Golden Gate bridge.

We painted it one more time: Demon Red, and outran every bike for blocks around. I'm remembering this now because it was Christmas time. Somehow we must have come into some extra money that year. Or maybe it was just time to do something extra special for Sis.

Anyway, come Christmas morning there was a brand spankin' new girl's bike under the tree for our sister. It was royal blue and although it wasn't the Red Demon, we allowed as it was a pretty good bike for a girl. We did, of course, plan to sneak a ride or two on it. This was to be Teddy's last Christmas with us, but we didn't know that then.

We were pretty careless I guess, but in those days things were hardly ever stolen. Not big things anyway, such as bikes. We just sort of figured it wouldn't happen to us.

It was evening and just a couple of days after Christmas and we were home alone, just us kids, gathered around the gas-fired imitation fireplace. We were sitting around the radio taking in one of the good old radio shows.

Teddy was in his usual spot beside me and all of a sudden his hackles were up and so was he. The low deep-in-the-throat growl should have been all the warning we needed. We ignored it, just as readily as we did his pacing at the front door. Like I said, a watchdog is no better than his human counterparts and we utterly failed to heed his warnings. Naturally, the new bike disappeared.

I suppose that old saw about love being blind is not only true but it also has deeper implications than just a casual reference to surface beauty. It's about the only explanation that I can give for what transpired the following summer.

To us, Teddy was admirable in all his traits. Probably he did a lot of things that were offensive to others. In many ways, he must not have been the perfect dog when viewed from an adult's perspective.

Being just kids, we could find no fault in Ted. But parents need to be more aware of the potential for problems that dogs represent and must pass on to their children these concerns in advance of an actual occurrence. In that manner children can recognize that some behaviors are not cute to others but are instead, offensive. After all, it is the kids who spend most of the time with a dog. I'm not blaming Mom and Dad for what happened. I'm just making an observation.

Early one evening of that summer so long ago, Teddy became ill and began to act most strange but he did not appear to be sick in the usual sense. I'll skip the details, as it is still not too pleasant to recall.

But Teddy did not last through the night and I only wish to this day that whoever fed him ground glass in hamburger would have had to watch him die, or witness my tears. That would have been punishment enough.

Farewell Teddy.

"The doggie-door to Heaven
is always open."

THE WAR ON DRUGS

*The hard-ribbed steel bed of the canopied truck
was beating my butt to jelly and my hip joints
were starting to ache. The early morning air was
crisp and cold in my lungs. We were doing at
least 40 miles per hour on a dirt trail that was
better suited for slow walking than fast driving.
We were on a drug bust and I was nervous.*

THE MARIJUANA FARM was on the top of a mountain, a spot
which offered the occupants a 360-degree view of the terrain and
anybody coming up to visit. And we were coming up fast in a
cavalry-like charge excepting that our mounts had wheels instead
of hooves. But the ride was just as rough.

Twelve very well-armed men filled the trucks churning up
the road to the marijuana farm. Ben and I had a special assignment: Keep the six packs of dogs occupied while the guys with the
drawn guns took care of the ranchers. Eighteen dogs in all were
reported at the site. Ben and I had worked out our strategy for
our portion of the raid after yesterday's briefing.

The campsite, that is, the marijuana farm, had been sur-
veyed earlier by a binoculared snoop from an adjacent mountain
top. A small unmarked private airplane with a Drug Enforcement
Officer on board had made a couple of fly-overs earlier as well.
Any more surveillance might have tipped off the ranchers that
something was up, so the team was going with what information
they had from those two sources.

The eighteen or so dogs on the hilltop pretty much eliminated any total surprise tactics, thus, the headlong rush up the hillside.

The dogs included a large white wolf type animal, a Shepherd or two and a Pit Bull. Ben and I agreed to bail out of the trucks, keep our heads down and hopefully out of the line of fire, should there be any, and go for the two most aggressive dogs. One each. To the rest of the canines, we could only offer our behinds and hope for the best.

This was not my first drug bust. The War on Drugs had produced special teams whose jobs varied from street arrests, undercover penetrations, interdiction of supplies, recruitment of informers and so on right up to assault groups. This was an assault group.

Usually, I am keyed up and excited but not particularly frightened. We dogcatchers tend to keep a low profile during these exercises. This time I was genuinely nervous. Twelve guys with bulletproof vests and a small arsenal of weapons tend to do that.

Four vehicles dashed onto the flat area around the campsite, fanned out in a surround pattern and braked to a hard stop. Four dust plumes which had heretofore trailed behind the vehicles now rolled forward over the stopped cars and trucks. Great. Here's dirt in your eye.

Twelve troopers drew sidearms, shotguns or rifles and charged the aluminum-bodied travel trailer which served as home to the ranchers. We two unflak-jacketed Animal Control guys armed with dog leashes jumped into the fray.

Six men shouted six different commands to whomever was inside the trailer while six other guys milled around the complex, keeping a wary eye out for whatever. Two or three of the shouting six kept threatening to shoot the dogs if somebody didn't come out of the trailer in a hurry.

Pretty quick-like a guy showed up at the door, buck naked, obviously totally frightened and equally confused, yelling "Don't shoot my dogs!"

In the meantime the white wolflike dog decided that bravery was best displayed from a comfortable distance and took off. The Pit Bull was crippled, its back having at some time apparently been broken and it was all that he could do to scurry underneath the silver trailer where he commenced to put on an awesome display of ferocity. Only one dog offered any resistance and that was mostly vocal with a few halfhearted charges thrown in for effect.

Things soon settled down. A lady inside was brought outside after having been allowed to don a pair of pajamas. The now handcuffed naked man was brought a pair of shorts from the trailer, cuffs were temporarily removed and he was allowed to put on the shorts. He was then permitted to corral a barking dog and chain him up before being handcuffed again. It was all over but the paperwork. No one was shot, no dogs were dead and Ben and I both had unblemished butts.

We had one of the SWAT guys take us partway down the mountain to where we had parked our dog vans. Driving up the mountain, collecting the target dogs and making it back down again without getting stuck in the bottomless sand was the true miracle of the day.

The following morning, the guy on the hill showed up at the kennel to reclaim the only two dogs we had felt needed to be taken into custody after the arrest. The remaining sixteen or so stayed on the mountaintop. The owner, whose name was Ernie, was released on his own recognizance until trial day. They trusted him to show up on his own!

Ernie was, in reality, a pretty decent human being. He was not a prosperous citizen, to be sure, but admirable nevertheless. All those eighteen dogs in his possession were homeless mutts he had personally rescued and was caring for until he could find homes for them.

The reassessment: Twelve armed men, pumped up to a fever pitch, who assault a home and seriously risk injury to themselves or others, for the sake of capturing a couple of marijuana plants grown for personal use only. Could not one uniformed officer have simply walked up to the door, knocked, and said, "Now about those three plants you have..."

But this was the War on Drugs. Like they say, war is hell.

BOSS

A Pit Bull terrier known as 'Boss' was laid to rest today in the Sierra Vista Pet Cemetery. And so came to light the solution to a five-year mystery: Whatever became of Boss? Age caught up to him, as it does to all of us, and in the process solved the enigma of his disappearance.

SOME MIGHT FIND IT STRANGE to bury a pet with the same dignity and respect that is customarily reserved for humans. However, such is a fitting tribute to a dear friend and therefore, Boss lay in state in a cherrywood casket lined with white satin. His head reposed in final rest upon a satin pillow. With the ravages of time imprinted upon his body, even in death it was easy to see the magnificent creature that Boss had been in his prime. Once broad shouldered, deep chested and square jawed, there was still a hint of the bulging muscles that once layered his frame. Boss had truly been quite a figure.

Bruno, his owner, friend and companion for fifteen years, bid his last farewell and the coffin was closed and sealed. And I, standing nearby, could not help thinking that this single act finally closed the book on a puzzle that started so many seasons before.

That's when a Pit Bull attack had been reported on the south side of town, a rural area given to medium-size homes on large-size lots. I stopped at the reporting party's house and was met by a man nearly beside himself with rage and adrenaline flow. He roared and exploded, recounting how he had heard his cat screaming. He went to the back yard from where the sounds had emanated and found a Pit Bull standing over his now dead cat and challenging his dog, a small Heinz variety, which was yelping frantically at the Pit.

And, as he watched, the Pit turned his attention to the Heinz. In a flash, the two clashed but without intervention, the outcome was a foregone conclusion. Grabbing the nearest thing at hand, the man began to beat on the Pit. The flimsy grass rake he had grabbed was a poor weapon, to say the least. The rake soon snapped over the Bull's powerful back without inflicting any real damage whatsoever. Then for some unexplained reason, the Pit broke off the attack. This uncharacteristic behavior saved the life of the Heinz for it surely was no match for a determined and aroused Pit Bull terrier.

The Pit had turned away and left the area, walking as with a purpose but not in flight. It was as though he considered what had just happened as a minor incident and not something worth getting excited about.

The man quickly checked his dog for injuries and found that while he had been superficially bitten, none of the wounds were serious. He chucked the dog inside where he would be safe and went after the Pit.

By that time he was maniacally aroused and he pursued the Pit, totally without a plan, not knowing what he intended to do but certain that he would do something to stop the dog from doing more harm.

That's when he caught up with Boss as the dog angled across the street and almost immediately spied another dog. Boss went on the attack as soon as he saw the other dog. The pursuing gent, more enraged than ever, saw the attack begin and, shouting furiously, he charged toward the swirling mass of dog against dog. He hoped to accomplish with noise what he had previously failed to do with force. The noise availed him naught but at least it did alert the other dog's owner.

Reacting quickly, said owner grabbed a length of 2x4 off of a stack of lumber in the driveway. Although intended for new construction, he had momentarily found a better use for it. Acting coolly under the circumstances, he chose his swings carefully, like a batter at the plate. Once, and again, then again, he struck the Pit with sufficient force to maim or kill the average dog. The only result was that on the third strike the 2x4 snapped but by this time Boss had had enough. Tail tucked, he broke off the attack and headed for the sagebrush.

That was the account that I was able to construct from the witnesses when I arrived on the scene. Boss and his owner were identified by the two neighbors involved and a citation was issued to the Pit's owner. The charge was harboring a vicious and dangerous animal. Boss, however, was nowhere to be found.

His rampage had taken less than fifteen minutes and he left in his wake one dead cat, one dog requiring medical attention and another dog saved from injury only because its owner happened to be nearby and was quick to react.

I finished the citation and related reports and scoured the area for a couple of hours, crisscrossing every street two, three and four times without a sign of Boss. At every home where I found a dog outside, I stopped and warned the residents that a Pit was on the loose. The message was always the same: "Put your dog inside for the rest of the day and call me if you see a Pit in the area." Altogether I warned about fifteen persons and not one of them had seen Boss.

Over the next three days I patrolled the area heavily. I always stopped at Boss's house to see if Bruno, his owner, had seen the dog and each time he assured me that he had not seen Boss since the day of the incident. I believed him.

On the fourth day following the attack I got my first lead. At a local service station I interviewed the operator who informed me that he had been fishing the previous day and had seen what appeared to be a dead dog caught up in a mass of driftwood lodged on a sandbar in the middle of the river. He could not tell for sure but he thought that it might be a Pit Bull.

He gave me a good description of the area along the river where he had seen the dog and I was relatively certain that I could drive within a mile or so of the spot and then find it on foot from that point.

That afternoon my supervisor and I bounced along the rough dirt road bordering the river, watching as we went. When we got to the area where we thought the dog might be, we got out and started walking the grounds. We checked both banks as we trudged and scrutinized all of the sandbars. The river was running high for that time of year so there was a lot of debris to scan.

About 500 yards from the start, we found what we were looking for. In the middle of the stream, on a sandbar jammed with brush, tree limbs, plastic bags and other trash, we could see a half submerged fawn-colored dog. The river was running far too fast to attempt to retrieve the dog, but it did appear to be Boss.

That sighting would suggest that it had been there for a few days. The timing was right and the repeated blows on Boss's body were certainly enough to have caused his death. It could also be likely that one of the embittered neighbors had killed the dog and then intentionally neglected to tell us about it. At any rate, we did conclude from the available evidence that the case could be closed.

And, it might have been, so far as I was concerned, but it was far from over for someone else. It might have been one of the two owners whose pets had been involved in the attacks. Or it could have been any one of the fifteen or so people whom I had warned about the loose Pit Bull. In any event, one or more of the people living in the neighborhood accused me of bungling the investigation. One of them at least, went so far as to implicate me in a supposed collaboration with the Pit Bull's owner, Bruno, in order to get him off the hook with minimum damage. It was implied that I was a good friend of Bruno's and was close enough to him to be a frequent luncheon guest, at Bruno's expense. Or so it was alleged.

The matter went all the way to the City Manager himself who came out to interview me, privately, so that I could explain my side of the allegations. I assured him that prior to the incident I had never met this Bruno person; further that I had scrupulously followed established procedure in issuing the citation with the appropriate charges based on eyewitness reports; and finally that I could not move to a court of appropriate authority to have the dog destroyed as it appeared that the dog had disappeared and was in fact dead. What else could I do?

The assumption of death was, of course, based on the sighting at the river and the fact that no one had seen the dog since the incident. I managed to convince the City Manager that everything was on the up and up and once again, I felt that the case was closed. Or so I thought.

The months that followed were full of the normal everyday stuff of animal control. As an interesting sidelight to the drama, there happened an ironic twist of fate. The gentleman who owned the cat that Boss had killed bought a new dog. And guess what? The dog bit the paperboy. Now it may be Okay for a dog to bite the dogcatcher and a dog might get away with biting the meter reader or the cable guy. But never, never bite the postman. The postman is the ultimate no-no bite target but paperboys are acceptable, after a fashion. So he bit the paper carrier.

The new dog so acquired was an Australian Shepherd. The Aussie is not generally vicious by nature but is well noted for quickness in nipping when needed to protect his turf or his charges. The dog is, after all, a shepherd and his job is to protect the flock and to control its movements. He does this in a variety of ways and is an excellent working dog. One of the ways in which he works is to nip at the heels of any member of his flock that goes astray.

He is territorial as well and his land is his land and you ain't welcome unless invited. And should you have the audacity to enter upon his land anyway, he will escort you out. These mannerisms can be tempered to a great extent by proper training and socialization and thereafter the Aussie is a wonderful pet.

In the instant case however, the dog was still young and not yet conditioned and the paper boy got nipped as he was beating a hasty retreat following an aborted attempt to deliver the newspaper.

The case was handled fairly with all due regard for the legalities required but not with a great deal of warmth or sympathy for the dog's owner.

Three years after the Boss incident, Bruno's new dog, Sugar by name, was buried in the Pet Cemetery. For my part, I had pretty much forgotten all about the affair, but Sugar brought it all back to mind for she too, was a Pit Bull terrier.

Bruno is not a big man but he is powerfully built, muscular, like his dogs. I don't know if his now-grayed hair was red but he gives that impression, with a temper to match. He was once a professional boxer with some one hundred fights under his belt. He probably had several more nonprofessional bouts as well, and was not the kind of guy you would consider as sentimental. But as Sugar was placed into the grave, tears rolled down Bruno's husky cheeks as he wept openly and unabashedly with grief over the loss of his pet. And I gained new insight into Bruno's character.

I knew that at that moment I could have reopened the episode of Boss and that I would have received the whole, unvarnished truth. In spite of the evidence, I had always felt that Boss had not died in the river. Call it a sixth sense, but I was never truly satisfied with the conclusions we had reached, even though there was not then, nor later, anything to show otherwise. But this was not the time to open old wounds. The present ones were painful enough for Bruno so I let it pass.

It was nearly five years later that Boss was laid to rest beside Sugar and the past was now present. The chronicle had to have a period affixed and at long last, the truth would do just that.

Boss, it seems, went to California that very night of the attack, driven by Bruno who traveled all night, round trip, so that Boss would be beyond the reach of all who might wish him harm. And so that he himself would not be missed, Bruno returned immediately.

Actually, he never really lied to me. He only failed to tell the whole truth. He repeatedly assured me, when asked about Boss, that he had not seen him since the night of the incident. And that was true. I guess I never asked the right questions or asked the questions in the right way. If I had, I think Bruno would have answered truthfully, for he is that kind of man. He has respect for his word but also great love for his dog. Thus, in the absence of that most specific and direct query, he simply failed to elaborate or clarify his answers.

And so the book finally closed on Boss and Bruno.

"Tiptoe...sleeping dogs have
been known to lie..."

MOCHA TAKES A POWDER

Unless you're from another planet, you know that Nevada is a gamblin' state. We call it Nevada style gaming but it's a bit more than just fun and games for some people. One of the most common postcards available to send the folks back home pictures a burro. The caption says, "I lost my A-- in Nevada."

BUT THERE'S A FELLA who lost more than that in Nevada. He lost a cute little Putty Tat, a valued black and white feline all decked out in a pink collar and red harness. She was living with her owner, Kent, in a motor home parked in a special section reserved for such temporary habitation at a local casino.

One day she took off and some days later poor Kent had to do the same, but without his beloved cat. Before he left, Kent hung a bunch of lost cat posters around the area and even offered a reward. But alas, no cat, even though numerous people kept saying "I t'ought I taw a Puddy Tat."

We set up box traps in the area and questioned people who camped there in the parking lot, plus the few folks who had homes surrounding the lot. But still no luck. We gave up and I think Kent did too because he stopped calling.

That's when Lady Luck played a hand. One bright sunny day the cat showed up by surprise in this guy's Volkswagen bus. We got the cat out from its hiding place and it apparently was the missing feline all right. She had lost the harness but still wore her pink collar.

But there was another problem. All of Kent's notices were long gone and we didn't have a phone number for him. So we had a cat but not a Kent. What to do?

Someone remembered that Kent had placed a lost ad in the local newspaper so we persuaded them to back-check the classifieds. We were likewise busy going through our past records but with little luck.

Then there was this lovely lady who lived across the street from the lot where Kent had parked. She just happened to be an animal lover. She also just happened to be the wife of the guy who owned the Volkswagen where the kitten was found hiding, and was one of the persons who assisted in our attempts to trap the furtive feline, she being a very involved person.

She also happened, like a blessed pack rat, to have stashed away one of the original, genuine, handwritten lost posters autographed by none other than Kent himself. From that we obtained his phone number. And in a couple of days we saw a delightful reunion.

THAT CASINO PARKING LOT also figured in another episode involving a cat. This one included a motorhome too. In this case the cat did not escape or get lost. It was just picked up as a protective custody impound.

It appears the cat's owner shot herself. It is not known how she managed that but presumably she just pointed the gun at herself and pulled the trigger. There was no one else present at the time and no indication that the gun went off by itself. What wasn't clear was if she meant to do it. Scuttlebutt had it that it was an attempted suicide.

The oddity of the situation was that, as she was wheeled into emergency surgery, she pleaded with members of the hospital staff to save her cat. So we did. At least we tried.

Since we had no record of a next of kin to take over, we kept the cat for quite some time. Too long, as a matter of fact, for one day when we made another call to the hospital to see how the lady was doing, she was gone. So was her motorhome. But she made no effort to reclaim her cat. I could not believe that she, whose last words from the gurney concerned her beloved pet, would have split and abandoned her pet. But she did.

We never did learn the cat's name but I called her Nugget. She was a lovely little calico and I was sorta hung up on her. Disappointed at her owner's disappearance, and involved with the little darling day to day at the shelter, I had quite an emotional investment in her and so, suckered again, I took her home.

That's when I learned a good lesson.

At that point I already had a favored Siamese cat. He was a delightful blend of rich dark coffee, smoothed out with a single dose of real cream. Hence we named him Mocha. Mocha was not only Siamese in nature but also in breed.

The Siamese are rulers. Furthermore, they have grown accustomed to the role over many generations. Their imperial airs and haughty expressions come quite naturally to them and, if their wish is to remain above the commoners, they do so with aplomb. Mocha did just that. He also declined to share his palace with Nugget, in his opinion, an unregal and unwelcome guest.

He terrorized Nugget and forbade her to ever enter a room in his presence. Hence she spent far more time under furniture than on it. Her time to prowl was when Mocha took a nap or a stroll outside. Otherwise, she hid out.

How does one train a cat? It can be done because we have all seen trained cats on TV. But this old dogcatcher certainly does not know how it is done. And try as I might, Mocha, the night stalker, would not change. So it turned out that Nugget's trials were not yet over. She had to be returned to the pound to await her turn at the if-and-when of adoption. But luck prevailed. She got to keep her name plus an enthusiastic new owner. Nugget was finally free to roam new premises devoid of her Mocha nemesis.

But he was still up to his old tricks. Figuratively speaking, Mocha had a red bandanna packed with a few travel goodies tied to the end of a short stick stuck in a corner of the closet. It was there as a reminder to us not to ever again violate the sanctity of his home by allowing another intruder to invade his premises.

We, his lowly humans, certainly got the message after he had laid siege to the entire house during Nugget's prolonged but unsuccessful attempt to become a member of the household. It was his symbol of tyranny, an emblem of the power he held as Master of the house. It served to remind us that there were to be no others put before him.

It was also Mocha's pronouncement that bedraggled stray dogs were unwelcome. Ditto winged creatures with ruffled feathers or bent beaks. The doors to his house only opened out, so saith Mocha the Mighty.

We really did try to honor his wishes, more to save our sanity than his vanity, although we thought it a bit presumptuous of him to declare them so boldly. And then one day the unthinkable happened.

Rain pelted down with such force that small limbs were wrenched from the trees, flowers bent and broke under the relentless onslaught. Gutters soon ran full and water stood inches deep in the streets, patiently waiting for the drains to do their jobs.

Predictably, the phone rang with its insistent demand: answer me, answer me. It seems that there was this dog that had taken up a spot on the porch by the front door of a home that was not his. He was there. He did not move. He merely quivered.

The report was that it was presumably an injured dog at a residence and that he had probably been hit by a car in the blinding rain. It is our duty to respond to all calls purporting to involve an injured animal.

Oftentimes the Sheriff's Office will assist us by checking out the report firsthand and then, if it is valid, will pass it on to us. That night however, they were too busy with numerous car crashes. It was one of those reports that had to be taken at face value.

In short order I was at the residence where the injured dog was reportedly hanging out. However, I was alone because the dog was no longer there. He had taken off so apparently he wasn't all that injured, if at all.

I, on the other hand, felt like a refugee from Noah's Ark, soaked through and through, even though I had been exposed only briefly to the downpour. My thoughts went to the dog and I imagined him wet and cold. I resolved to take a few more minutes to look for him, even though he was now presumed uninjured but was probably just wet and frightened by the flashes of lightning and accompanying bass rumble of thunder.

Wipers waged a futile battle against the rain which poured over the windshield in sheets rather than drops. If possible, the downpour had gotten worse. Visibility was zip so that the window had to come down if I were to see to drive. Anyone watching would have been amused by this idiot creeping down the street with a window down and a rain-soaked head poked outside the vehicle. Silly, but it worked.

That's when a rolling ball of water broke loose from the side of the road and angled toward my slow moving vehicle. It looked like Surf's Up at Waikiki, except that the wave cresting toward me was more like a ball than a wave's curl.

It was soon apparent that the ball of water contained a dog like the nucleus of a cell. Droplets flew from him in every direction as he ran and created the ball-like illusion.

And then the ball bounced and I wound up with the front half of a dog in my lap and the back half hanging out the side of the open window. Any dry spot I might have had left on me soon disappeared. I braked the car to a halt and then hauled the dog completely inside and finally drove both of us home.

Mocha did the arched back, fluffed hair, erect tail hissy-fit routine as soon as we walked in the back door and I knew this was not a cat-dog marriage made in heaven. The dog was not only terrified, but wet, and possibly injured.

Have you ever smelled a wet sheep dog? Ten towels later and a floor mopping in the utility room revealed I indeed had an Old English Sheep in tow. I always thought those guys were supposed to be immune to rain. How do they guard flocks and chase wolves if they can't stand a touch of rain?

The next morning the dog went with me to the pound and stayed there when I came home. And the corner of the closet stood starkly empty. No stick on a bandanna. Also, no Mocha.

I gave him another 24 hours to come home on his own before I went looking for him. The little ingrate had done this once before over a similar matter and I had a feeling that I knew exactly where he had gone. He had it made there during his last disappearance and I suspected he remembered the good times. Mocha had come to us a deserted little ball of Siamese fur and we had mothered him into a fine specimen of his breed. And this was how we were to be repaid. Ha!

When he utterly failed to show up at home, I followed my hunch. Sure enough, that is where he went, back to the good life, where no Nugget kittens or wet sheep dogs would invade.

It was time to do the bumper sticker thing: Let it go. Mocha, it seems, had wormed his way into the good graces of not one, but three homes a couple of blocks up the street. He took the corner house by storm and then assaulted the other homes on either side. He showed up at each home in turn and inquired into the menu of the day. Then he would pick and choose his catch. They all loved him and were happy to see him return.

We did what prudence said to do. We let Mocha go. I knew that some time soon I would probably bring something home again and Mocha would get bent all out of shape and abandon ship once more. Mocha apparently had it made where he was.

I offered to foot any medical bills that might come up or to find another home for him if it shouldn't work out. Mocha was also Glenna's favorite cat and it was tough on her, much more so than it was for me, but she did her duty as she saw it and also let him go.

So far as we know, Mocha lived the rest of his life there on the corner, no doubt regally.

"Now remember...cats really are
supreme beings, but humans
own the can openers..."

AN OLD SOFTIE

It is not uncommon for a physician to report a case of suspected child abuse to the authorities. As a matter of fact, it is the law.

It is common because in most cases of abuse, the child eventually winds up in an emergency room for treatment. There, the doctor sees the injury and reports it.

Why do child abusers take the victimized child to a doctor? Who knows? Perhaps the fear of discovery and punishment would be more severe if it were initially hidden. Maybe it is remorse? Maybe the abusers think the cause of the injury won't be discovered? That the child really did fall down the stairs six times? Anyway, the child is brought in, the deed discerned and the report made.

It is different with animals.

MOST ANIMAL ABUSERS do not take their victims to the vet so it was a bit unusual for the Collie to wind up at the animal hospital, and more so because the owners had brought it in.

They claim they did so because it smelled. The hospital in question has a grooming business on the premises so that part of the story made sense. The dog needed grooming, they thought. They said so. Why else would it stink so badly?

The odor of gangrene on a living creature has an unmistakable scent that is unforgettable. And this Collie had it.

The veterinarian, upon discovering the cause of the rank stench, held off on treatment until the Humane Society could be contacted to witness and investigate the cause. Even though I was one of the new guys on duty, having just recently been hired, I got the assignment, along with a more seasoned officer.

Upon arrival we were escorted back to one of the examining rooms in the rear portion of the building. Our subject was a beautiful sable Collie. She had a twinkle in her eyes and a twitch to her tail which told us that whatever experiences she had undergone had failed to destroy her spirit.

It took only a moment to see the problem. The poor dog had been chained up in the back yard for a considerable period of time. Furthermore, she had either been chained before she reached her full growth or the choke chain was too tight the day they put it on her.

In the first place, she should not have been confined with a choker. They are training devices only, not collars. They are used just temporarily for training sessions, then removed. They are not intended for use as permanent restraint.

And the beautiful Collie was living proof of that logic. Her choke chain was firmly imbedded in the flesh of her neck, all the way around, except for a space of about two inches at the bottom of her throat. The chain had created a great gaping wound which was fully infected. The process was slow as the neck grew into the collar, ever tighter and tighter, until the resulting wound finally burst open and enmeshed flesh and chain into one. That's when the gangrene set in.

This could never have happened to a dog that was loved, handled and played with on a daily basis. Not only would the tight chain have been noticed but the wound itself would have been evident. It just should not have happened to the beautiful Collie and if we had our way, it would never happen again.

There was little we officers could do in the instant case to prevent a repeat except to deny the dog to its owners. So we started the process which we hoped would result in a court order to prohibit them from retrieving the dog.

The Humane Society agreed to bear the costs of corrective surgery and the choke chain was cut out of the flesh and the wound properly closed. The nature of the wound and its cause and treatment were carefully photographed and documented. All hospital records were copied and included in the official report.

Next, two officers went to the owner's residence and interrogated them. After reading them their rights, as required by the Miranda ruling, a citation was issued charging them with neglect and abuse, two counts. Notes were taken on the conversations with family members and a sketch was made of the yard where the dog was kept. The location and length of the chain was also noted. All this was turned over to the director of the Society.

It was her job to determine two things: First, was the action in denying property to the owners proper and legal? This is the due process provision. Second, could we prove our case? She determined that we could.

Then there is the Constitution of the United States which provides that none may be deprived of property without due process. In most instances, this means by a court judgment, sometimes after a jury trial and at other times by a judge sitting alone.

In this instance, the director of the Humane Society had been empowered to sit as a hearing officer much the same way as a judge would have but only without all the judicial formality and restrictive rules. It was more like a conference.

Witnesses were called and testimony taken, just as in a trial. The owners were present and were allowed to make a case as to why they should not be denied the right to their property. Once a decision is reached, if the owner loses, he has the right to appeal for a stay of judgment and instructions are given in detail as to how this can be accomplished.

It is quite a simple process and if followed, puts everything on hold. The appeals judge then evaluates all of the evidence and will either deny or uphold the hearing officer's decision.

If upheld, the defendant can then ask for a retrial if the decision is not acceptable. All this procedure becomes a bit more lengthy than a trial would be. Most often, the director's decision is accepted by the defendants. This speaks well for the quality of the director's judgment. In other words, if the director says the defendants are guilty, they usually are and they know it. So they either agree with the decision immediately or they allow it to stand by default. If they do not appeal, it so stands.

That is what happened in the instant case. The owners objected to the ruling but failed to appeal so the judgment stood and the dog was not given back.

What did happen to the dog? The Humane Society had a foster home program for exceptional critters, assuming of course that there are enough foster homes to fill the needs of deserving animals. The sad truth is that all too often there are not enough homes.

The idea of fostering an animal is parallel to that of giving refuge to foster children. A dog or other animal is fostered until a prospective new owner comes along and then if it all works out according to Hoyle, the pet is relinquished to the new home. Foster tenders are thus heroes and heroines. Trust me.

Fostering, of course, also involves that time-honored relinquishment, painful though it may be. "Let it go." That's fostering. It is hard to do and Nell, the consummate Animal Control Officer, fostered the beautiful Collie, for what turned out to be the rest of its life. Confidentially, I don't think for a minute that there were no other opportunities for adoption. No way. No iron curtain. Nell just turned soft, that's all. It was a good match.

FRIENDS

MOST ANIMAL CONTROL OFFICERS like dogs. Most are pet owners themselves. So it is only natural, in the course of our daily rounds, that we meet and become personal friends with a number of dogs living in the community. I know a lot of them, both by sight and name, know where they live, and have a nodding acquaintance with their owners.

Some of them we meet because we come into contact with them in an official capacity. Some were former inmates of the kennel, that is, they were adopted from the Shelter. These are always favorites. Some just sit in their yards gleefully greeting passersby and we stop and get acquainted.

There is one black Lab named Gofer I happened to meet that way because that's what he does. Throw a ball or stick and he will go for it, endlessly.

He has a number of tennis balls lying around his yard and if you even look favorably at him, he will go get one and give it to you to throw. He expects you to be smart enough to toss it and if you are, he will dutifully go get it and drop it at your feet for a repeat performance. He'll play catch and fetch for as long as you will. Afterward, both of you will feel better for it. His owner recently put up a railway crossing style sign that reads 'CAUTION— LAB CROSSING.'

THEN THERE IS OTIS just down the street from me. I see him whenever I take a walk in his direction. No, he's not an elevator but he is a Rottweiler, and a really exceptional example of what the breed ought to be.

On the way to his house I pass the home of Maggie, a Labrador Retriever of the chocolate variety. Frisky and full of fun, she is in training to be a hunting dog. She is progressing quite favorably, might I add. Sometimes her zest for life causes her to forget some of the finer aspects of her training but she is young. She'll learn.

ZEUS is another Rottie I once met eyeball to eyeball over a fence at two in the morning. Zeus was doing a bit of barking and several people expected me to go into this dark yard and take him out. Zeus said no, and I agreed that the matter could wait until daylight. He no longer lives in our city but we became friends before he left. We meet now and again and it is always a warm moment when it is obvious that he remembers.

MANY TIMES Stella, my Sheltie, and I would walk out of our way to say Hi to Jackson, who was a Siberian with a thick, rich black and white coat covering a body that was all heart. Jacks would run back and forth along the low fence, cavorting with Stella, and after the initial excitement, he would come over and nose my outstretched hand, presenting his big woolly head for a hug and a rub.

Ominously, shortly after six o'clock one Monday morning my phone rang. A ringing phone at that hour almost always means that the Sheriff's Office dispatcher is calling and it is usually bad news of some sort.

This call was to report an injured dog that had been hit by a car and was down in the middle of our main artery. An officer was standing by to keep the dog from being struck again until I could arrive and take over.

It was winter and cold. I drove as fast as I could, peering through a gradually defrosting windshield. I had a sick feeling that I would know this dog when I got there but even with that premonition, I was not prepared to find this particular dog.

You have heard stories about police officers or ambulance drivers who arrive at an accident scene only to find that the victim is a known or loved individual. Well, it happened to me that morning. No, it was not one of mine. They were home and safe. But, it was one that I loved as though it were my own.

Jackson was not destined to make it but he remains to this day a favorite for many of us who were privileged to know him.

That big compound in the sky must be a delightful place. So many of our little friends are there.

"If he wants the ball so darned bad why doesn't he just keep it?"

AN ERROR

*The house was darkened again tonight. The front
yard was dappled with lights from the casino
across the narrow street and in the yard some
very young children played. But the house itself
was unlit. It occurred to me that it had been this
way every night for quite some time. Or at least so
it seemed.*

I HAD BEEN PASSING THIS CORNER on foot nightly since I had
decided to take up walking for exercise in the early evening.

The house was old. It was a leftover from the more prosperous
era of the west side neighborhood and although it was not on the
list of historical homes, it was nevertheless a stately place. Just
badly worn.

Commercialism had altered the residential character of the
area and left but a few of the older places intact as homes and most
of those were of the simpler, less grand style of that period. The
remaining prestigious dwellings housed professional offices. Only a
few remained that were still used for residential purposes. No longer
prime properties, they served as moderately priced housing until
such time as the growth of commerce would make the land itself
valuable enough to sell. When that time came, the house would most
likely be demolished to make way for a new office building.

Not a blade of grass grew, front or back, and the ground itself
had the same worn and tired look as the house in question. I
wondered if the occupants were themselves as worn and tired. And
possibly poor. The old place had piqued my interest and I knew that
I would follow its fortunes in the future.

In the ensuing days I casually observed the house in my passings. A couple of times I detected what appeared to be a dim light, as if from a candle or kerosene lamp inside. It could have been a very low wattage bulb but I did not think so. Why bother with an electric light too dim to be practical? The cost of a single light would not increase much if it were brighter. Then my interest gradually waned as no new insights were offered and I ceased to pay much attention to the place.

Soon the evenings began to cool and I quit walking in favor of indoor exercise so I no longer noticed the place or wondered about the dim light. It was, however, to play a role in future events, a role that in my wildest imagination I would not have conjured.

Rabies is a viral disease, that is, it is caused by a virus, its name stemming from a Latin word meaning rage or fury. And there is a form of rabies which induces a state of fury in an infected animal, a condition which causes it to bite and snap at any outside stimuli. One of its symptoms is constriction of the throat muscles which causes the animal to shy away from drinking, thus the disease is also known as hydrophobia, a fear of water.

In its final stages, there is no treatment and the victim faces almost certain death. There is no cure. However, it can be successfully treated in the early stages immediately following infection.

The most common cause of infection is a bite from a rabid animal which allows the disease carried in the animal's saliva to enter the bloodstream of the victim. Many mammals are capable of carrying the disease, the most common being bats, skunks, raccoons and foxes.

While most dogs do not contract rabies, they are nevertheless the most likely carriers to infect humans. This is simply because they are the animal most likely to bite a human due to their accessibility to their owners. Most of us do not have daily contact with foxes, for example, and are thus not likely to be infected by them.

Essentially, rabies is not communicable until it arrives in the final stages of development in the infected, biting animal. It is therefore usually sufficient to quarantine such suspect for observation for a period of ten days for domestic animals such as dogs and cats, and fifteen days for wild creatures.

The diseased animal will die of a rabies infection within the quarantine period, usually about halfway through. So, generally speaking, if the biting animal lives through the quarantine period, it was not rabid to begin with and the victim is safe and does not have to undergo treatment.

Animal Control Officers deal with countless bite cases involving domestic dogs. Most are minor because dogs have been bred for years to be friends, not enemies. However, a dog will bite whenever it perceives a need to do so. When they do bite someone, the specter of rabies arises and the health issue must be addressed.

Bites that do not break the skin are of no consequence from a health or rabies standpoint. However, if the skin is broken, then an infection could have been passed and quarantine of the offender is then in order.

Animal Control Officers develop a pattern, based on experience, to ask certain questions, get certain answers and follow through with specific procedures. It becomes rather automatic.

For example, It can be difficult, if not impossible, to misquote the conditions of quarantine. It is like saying two plus two equal four. It is automatic and would require momentary concentration to give any other answer.

Summer had faded into fall and fall had given way to winter as it always does. Then the first warm days of spring descended when the dog bit.

Some children were again playing in the dappled light from the casino across the street amid the dusty dirt that still prevailed in the yard in front of the house with dim lights.

No one was ever able to say why the dog bit the kid. Maybe the child stepped on him in the dark or stumbled over him in play. Maybe the dog thought his youthful master was being attacked. No one knows why he bit but bite he did.

The dog was a German Shepherd. Probably he was a purebred. He looked it, but none knew for sure. He was just named Captain, or Cap for short. He was getting old, slow and dowdy-looking. And so if he once had good lines, they no longer showed. Maybe he was uncomfortable or in some pain due to his age. Maybe he was a grump and that was why he bit the boy.

AN ERROR

I anticipated that the dog probably would not be current on his shots. It just seemed economically unlikely and it turned out that was indeed the case. He hadn't had any shots since Hector was a pup and that meant that he would have to be placed in formal quarantine, in the Shelter under our observation for the requisite 10-day period. And so Captain was impounded for rabies quarantine.

No one ever came to visit him. No one phoned to see how he was doing. His tenth day of confinement arrived and he could have gone home, but no one came for him.

Then the eleventh day passed, and the twelfth joined in passing. Soon we were into the fourteenth day and the kennel was full to overflowing. We needed to make space for new arrivals as that is unfortunately the way animal control regulates overpopulation. Captain, along with others, was selected for euthanasia.

My supervisor reviewed the list and asked if there were any possibilities that Captain's owners would come for him. I could have saved him at that point but I thought back to that unlit house sitting cold and silent in the winter light. It seemed to me that there was simply no way that this family, unable to provide more than the barest of necessities, could possibly bail Captain out of jail and pay the fines and other attendant fees that were due.

On the fifteenth day Captain's mistress came to get him. She had understood me to say that the quarantine period was fourteen days.

Whose mistake was it? It doesn't really matter. That doesn't bring Captain back. I made a judgment call. It was wrong. Captain paid the price and I live with the consequences.

THE FUGITIVE

The high desert area of Nevada is somewhat different from the stereotypical desert usually envisioned when that word is mentioned.

WHILE ITS PREDOMINANT COLOR is tan, the vegetation is basically sagebrush and the soil is sandy, the overall impression being not really that of a desert. For one thing, the plant life is too abundant. For another, there are no sand dunes. Further, there are no cacti, or cactus, if you prefer.

Instead, here and there can be spotted a stunted kind of tree known as Pinion Pine. There is never any doubt that the area is arid but the inclination is to deny that it is truly desert country— more commonly known as *high* desert.

It is however, virtually impossible to walk in a straight line through this desert. The growth is quite abundant when viewed close up, resulting in a sort of serpentine path around the clumps of sage and tumbleweed. Thus, the eye can scan a large area while at the same time being unable to see much more than 10 or 15 feet straight ahead. It is this characteristic, this broken-field of vision that allowed Brown Dog to escape for so long.

The dog first came to our attention as the result of a some-what frantic call from Locust Drive, the paved portion of which ends about two city blocks from the next intersecting road. That final segment exists as a dirt road, bisecting two large areas of high desert.

The section farther to the west encompasses perhaps 10 acres while the eastern section includes about 20 acres before it joins what is literally the end of town. All in all, it is a large area to search.

It appears that the dog had spent the previous two evenings on the lawns of a couple of the houses bordering the desert. It also appeared that the dog was injured, ugly, emaciated, scruffy and altogether unwholesome in appearance. It was this latter quality that prompted the frantic calls, for they thought the dog might be rabid.

I refrained from saying all that I might have said since it seemed that the poor creature had been around for over a week in that condition. But it was only when the residents felt personally threatened that their humanitarianism surfaced.

Heaven only knows how long they would have waited to seek aid for the waif if they hadn't felt endangered. The moment they perceived a threat, they decided that the poor dog had to be picked up for its own good. Obviously, it had to be done, but not for the hypocritical reasons they espoused.

That first evening I patrolled the area on foot, looking for a sign that would help me locate and apprehend the dog. I found a couple of well established trails and two separate nesting areas, but no sign whatever of the dog. After an hour or so I gave up for the day.

The following morning the calls started again. The community was in danger. A rabid dog was loose. All the kids will be attacked and killed. Call out the militia.

All nonsense, of course. Dog-hunting in the heat of the day is stupid as no self-respecting dog is up and about then. They, being smart, prefer the early morning and early evening hours. It was not until evening of that day that I first saw Brown Dog.

My anger at those people returned the moment I laid eyes on the battered hulk of dogdom. The scrawny caricature of a dog had been in the area for over a week. Those people knew it but no one called or cared until they decided it was dangerous to have around.

His right rear leg was useless. He carried it over the rear of his left leg, except when running, at which time it just dangled. His skin was stretched taut over his bony skeleton. His eyes were the eyes of a wild beast that has been beaten into submission. Not proud, not defiant, just totally frightened and defeated.

I knew I had to catch him and that I had to end his misery, to erase it totally, for there was no return to whatever he had been. He wasn't going to make it easy though. He moved away constantly. He was wise and would not go anywhere but toward open space. There would be no cornering of this canny dog.

On the morning of the third day I shot at him with a tranquilizer gun but the dart struck a portion of an old barbed wire fence and ricocheted off into the desert. The rest of that morning was spent in a fruitless search through the shrubs and sage even though I knew he would no longer be up and about. The high desert defeated my best efforts to spot him again.

That afternoon, joined by two officers from the Sheriff's Department, I again combed, bush by bush, both areas adjoining Locust Drive. Nothing. It was as though the desert had allied itself with the dog. There were no fresh tracks on the trails he had previously used. The nesting areas had not been revisited. He was, for all practical purposes, gone. But I knew that he was not.

Again that evening, just before dark, I returned to the search. Most of my other duties were being assumed by my associate officer or just postponed altogether. Brown Dog had to be found.

On the morning of the fourth day the Governor's Office called to find out what was being done about catching the dog. By this time a half dozen families in the area were up in arms and someone among them had called the Governor to complain that not enough was being done to rid the neighborhood of this threat, even though no one admitted to seeing the dog again.

Obviously I could not capture something I could not even find. I think I walked two inches off of my already not-impressive height that day. I shifted the tranquilizer gun a thousand times, from left to right, from shoulder to shoulder, from two-hand carry to one-hand carry. It got heavier as the desert grew to astounding proportions, but still there was no sign of Brown Dog.

Once again, in the early evening, I found myself in the sagebrush. This time however, I had a plan. It seemed that I could not outsmart this critter. So maybe I could think like he was thinking.

If I were a dog, injured, tired, hungry, and hunted, where would I go to hide? I know enough about dogs to try to second-guess their reactions and patterns of behavior. I reasoned that a dog in such position would hide some place where it would not be seen. Also, that would be devoid of human scent, at least not a fresh trace.

It was obvious that he was not digging a nest under the brush for I had looked under every blankety-blank one of them. There weren't any drainage ditches or culverts in which to hide. There weren't any old or abandoned houses in the area.

But wait a minute. There was one old ranch site with outbuildings still in the area. The house was occupied but the outbuildings were deserted. And farther, just down the road, there were a couple of what were once detached garages. They needed checking. Yep, if I were a hunted three-legged dog, that's where I would be.

I checked all of them that day and didn't find a thing. I spoke to all of the owners and none had seen the dog. About this time I was really feeling worthless and not at all like the great white hunter. I called it quits.

But Glory be! It only took five minutes the next evening to find Brown Dog. I stumbled over an old chicken coop for about the umpteenth time but this time I decided to check inside. Sure enough, there in the corner crouched Brown Dog. He was pretty feeble and he could barely manage a deep growl and a show of teeth. I took him out as gently as I could. I believe that he was grateful when I administered that final injection. He had been so brave, so resilient. I always wish that I could just wave a magic wand and make everything all right for unfortunates such as Brown Dog.

ACE

It was the Christmas season, a time of miracles.
And Todd, the disheveled man, needed a miracle
to reclaim Ace, his constant companion. Their
sojourn was part comedy, part tragedy and
totally reflective of the furtive but valiant efforts
of a born loser in the game of life.

IT HAS BEEN SAID that a man and his money are soon parted but his dog is forever. If so, Todd, Hot Toddy, they called him, and his constant companion, Ace, were living proof of the adage.

Toddy had a buddy he called Bro, as a brother in spirit. But Toddy's significant partner in life was Ace, an unlikely mix of German Shepherd and Wirehaired Terrier. Toddy, his Bro and Ace lived in a tent down by the river. It was a secluded area because it was safer living on the river bank where they were seldom seen by others. That was a strategy in choice of living quarters, for Toddy, Bro and Ace were, in 1990s vernacular, homeless. On the riverbanks they would be less likely to be disturbed.

In a material sense, Ace was the most important possession in Toddy's meager household. And it is December when, with luck in winter, the daytime temperature might get all the way up to 40 degrees. At night it could dip down into the teens, which is why Toddy and Bro, with Ace in tow, could frequently be seen trudging their way into town from their secluded campsite on the river.

Once in town, they could get a hot meal for a small amount of dinero at one of the local casino restaurants, that is, if they had dinero. If not, they could get a once-a-day freebie meal at the Mission dining room set up for the less fortunate. And Toddy and Bro certainly could be numbered among those wanderers.

On occasion, if finding themselves with a few coins in pocket, they might indulge in a dose of adult beverage after a free meal. During those times Ace might be found tied up to some stationary object such as a sign post buried in concrete or a big green dumpster while waiting for Toddy and Bro to return and take him home.

Yes, it was true that sometimes the duo stayed away too long. And yes, it was true that Ace was often placed somewhere much too visible and too public, too subject to outside intervention. After all, how many good places are there to tie up a dog while tippling?

So, Ace would often wind up tied in some inappropriate place and, as Fate would have it, some well-intentioned citizen would espy Ace in his solitary confinement and telephone Animal Control. Upon receipt of the phone call, we would go out and arrest Ace and put him in doggy jail.

Toddy would eventually come out and discover his companion gone and would, in short order, show up at the kennel to reclaim him. This happened more than once and Toddy would plead poverty, which was true, and some arrangement would have to be made to bail out Ace. Toddy thus received numerous citations, paid impound fees, hocked some of his meager possessions to raise money, and who knows, maybe even pilfered something to garner funds.

At that stage, all our counseling efforts had been for naught because Ace continued to be tied up somewhere. Toddy said that he could not leave Ace behind at the campsite because the coyotes would dine upon him. And indeed, they would have. So, he asked us, what else was he to do? We didn't have a good answer.

Naturally, and inevitably, Ace ran afoul of Fate one time too often and he disappeared. His finders, it appeared, had taken matters into their own hands. They obviously weren't going to admit it either. It appeared that the saga of Ace, Toddy and Bro was over.

We looked for Ace. Toddy looked for Ace as did Bro but none of us could find him. Ace was generally nondescript, bigger than a small dog but a lot smaller than a big dog. He was mostly black with a little gray around the muzzle.

But he did have one distinguishing characteristic. Ace had endured some hardships from time to time. It is the price to pay when teamed up with a mostly homeless man. Ace had a hitch in his getalong and he sometimes acted like a tractor-trailer rig does when the trailer's brakes don't work too well. At such times the trailer starts to come around and run alongside the rig. Well, Ace did this too. Every few steps he would take a little skip-jump to allow his rear to synchronize with his front end. And every so often if that didn't work, he would bend in the middle as his rear tried to catch up with his front. He was a bit like Charlie Chaplin at such times but he was also totally identifiable as well.

Desperate, Toddy resorted to the press to get assistance in recovering Ace. Toddy said that he had spent more than $6,000 on Ace back when his financial circumstances were better, but that the money was not significant. The only thing that mattered was the return of his dog. Bro concurred. Christmas would not be the same without Ace to share the tent.

The press coverage gave us a lead but it was fairly slim. The owner of a local restaurant said a lady had approached him about the dog. She had noticed Ace tied up there for some time and asked the restaurateur if he knew who owned the dog. When told he did not, she proffered the remark that she would take it home and care for it. Apparently she did. December 8th was the date.

On the 18th the restaurant owner offered a free dinner to anyone who would reunite Ace and Toddy. He stated in the news-paper release that, having had a lot of dogs in his lifetime, he would hate to see the man and his dog separated.

The lady who rescued Ace responded to the press release by calling Animal Control. Her only concern was the welfare of the dog and she had no interest in dinner or reward. She just wanted assurance that the dog would receive adequate care.

There was no doubt that Toddy loved Ace and there was no doubt but that Ace reciprocated, as we had often seen the excitement in Ace when Toddy showed up to bail him out. If you have ever loved a dog, you will know and understand the feeling of companionship and love. You will also know and understand the gut-wrenching desolation that results from a loss of that relationship.

Sure, Toddy had it rough down by the river in a tent. But does that hardship really matter to a dog? A dog likes to be reasonably warm, decently fed and tremendously loved. Ace had all of that, even though there are many who would say that Ace had a dog's life and no dog should have to live like that. Excuse me, but that is often what dogs do. By what standards are we to judge? And how are we to convince a counselor, a lover of animals, a rescuer, that Ace was better off at the river than in her home?

I certainly was not equipped to be so persuasive but nevertheless I disagreed with the lady and stood with Toddy.

Apparently, although reluctantly, the lady finally agreed and relented in her insistence that she could do better by Ace than Toddy could.

In short order Ace and Toddy were reunited, but with one stipulation: Toddy was undergoing treatment by a local doctor and the process was nearly over. The agreement was that as soon as his medical needs were satisfied both Toddy and Ace would do like the birds: fly south for the winter. He did, they did. By the turn of the year both were gone and neither has ever been heard from again at the Shelter.

"I am not a common mongrel. My family
has merely been randomly bred!"

WRONG NUMBER

"ADAM CHARLES ONE and Adam Charles Three," intoned my van's radio. Ben, my fellow officer on duty that day, no doubt had the same message coming over his radio.

He responded first with "Adam Charles Three" and I followed on his verbal heels with "Adam Charles One." They had called. We had answered. Now it was their turn to talk again and it was not long in coming.

"Adam Charles One and Three, 10-5 with units, Spring Creek and Center."

We responded with "10-4 One clear," and "10-4 Three clear."

All that simply meant that the Sheriff's Office dispatchers had called Animal Control requesting that we meet with one or more cars from the Sheriff's Office at the intersection noted.

We in turn had acknowledged receipt of the transmissions and since we did not reply in the negative, the indication was that it was our intention to comply. That is one of the beauties of the Ten Code. It simplifies matters.

It was however, a bit unusual for them to request two officers. Ben was in a separate unit and was working on a different part of town. It just happened that he was in the section closest to the meeting place. We normally do not ride together in the same vehicle. That is SOP, or standard operating procedure, as we used to say in the military.

The request for two of us was tantalizing and aroused our curiosity. That was my mood as I turned around and headed for the designated site. Ben was waiting for me when I arrived. None of the other units were there and I reached for the microphone to advise dispatch that we were both in place. Just then a voice came over the radio saying, "All units: maintain radio silence."

There is a good reason for that procedure. There are a number of people in every community who enjoy listening to the police and fire calls on radio receivers known as scanners, which are for listening only as they do not have broadcast capability. They are called scanners since they have a signal-seeking function that does not stay on one single channel.

Rather, the scanner function roams the wave lengths looking for a strong signal, much like a bored TV watcher clicking the remote. When the scanner hits a signal, it stops and locks onto it until the traffic stops and then it resumes looking for action elsewhere. Via this operation, listeners can catch all the action from whatever source it originates. They can thus bounce from a fire call to a police call to a traffic stop by the highway patrol.

Criminals and other bad guys also own scanners but they don't use them for personal entertainment. They like to comb the airwaves so they can hear when the cops are onto their trail and scoot before officers can arrive.

To counteract the bad guys, the police use channels that are closed to the public. Naturally, the crooks buy those channels on the black market and thus it all goes back to Square One. The only safe way for police officers to protect themselves from snoopers is to say nothing during transmissions. Thus, the request for radio silence. The police obviously felt that the bad guys might be listening in.

But what would they be listening to? I was getting more interested in this development by the minute. I no sooner parked the van than three other units pulled up. Two were black and whites and one was unmarked.

That meant a detective was on the job. The unmarked car was a two-man unit and that often meant drugs but I was uncertain about that in the instant case. Apprehension mounted because druggies often have guns and dogs and such stuff.

Because of that hazard, briefings are usually held so that everyone involved has a role and also knows the roles of others involved. That tells everyone where everyone else is and how not to get shot.

But since it was not a drug bust, what was it?

It appears that there was this guy who was jamming the 9-1-1 line by calling and hanging up and then doing it all over again. And again. And again. He had been doing that off and on for three days until the police had finally managed to trace the calls.

They phoned him back and gave him a huge break. They didn't arrest him on the spot but they did advise that they would, posthaste, if he continued his little game. He continued. And that was why we were all gathered there on the corner.

We held a little roadside conference to discuss how we were going to go about the arrest. The officers had advance notice that the caller had two big dogs in his mobile home. One was reported to be a large German Shepherd and other was a Doberman Pinscher.

None of the officers wished to be bothered by the critters while they were apprehending the caller and that was why Ben and I were there. We were going to go in first and take the dogs outside and then everybody else would go in and capture the caller. No one knew for certain if the emotionally disturbed man might react violently. Ben and I must have parked our brains in the van for we thought that this was a good plan. But in essence, the plan was as nutty as the caller but neither Ben nor I tripped to it at the time.

Soon our little convoy arrived in front of the home and spread out along the street and drive. It was getting a bit dim out but yet a long way from dark and we did not want to go too slowly just in case it got too dark too quickly.

We all took up our positions and more or less surrounded the home. We beat on the walls and on the door with our night-sticks and yelled "Police. Open up," and so on.

Well, if I were inside, I'd be scared to death to open a door. The man inside probably was too, because he didn't show up and he didn't open the door.

Two officers flanked the front door and two others covered the rear window and the back door.

The front door had a little porch with a tiny roof over it and offered very little space for anyone to stand on. The two guys flanking either side of the front door did an iffy job of it, due to the restricted space, doing the best they could under the circumstances.

The other two guys had plenty of room in which to move around. The sergeant stayed out in the car parked at the end of the driveway, with a rifle stuck out the side window. It gave him a better field of fire, he explained later.

But frankly, he was more than a bit concerned about the dogs. He was always concerned about dogs, especially big dogs and more so when one was a big German Shepherd and the other was a big Doberman like the ones inside that trailer.

I have seen that Sergeant tackle a pothead twice his size and half his age and never use his nightstick or draw his gun. He's fearless in such situations and has no concern whatever for his own safety. But mention dogs and Sarge will take a back seat to the action. And that's okay by me because I can't do what he does so well either.

Our first obstacle was encountered almost immediately. The door was locked and the caller inside was obviously not going to unlock it. We stood on that little back porch and pondered a bit when I happened to notice a shovel leaning against the wall just beyond the small porch. I motioned to the officers to stay put and I began to pry open the door.

I had no sooner started when something happened. The little doggy door at the bottom of the people door moved. So did two officers. They practically levitated. At one moment they stood firmly on the ground and in the next instant they were both in the bed of a pickup truck that was parked at the end of the driveway. The truck was about twelve feet away from where they were standing before the doggy door moved and suddenly they were in the truck, in the conventional ready stance with knees slightly bent and guns drawn and pointed toward the sky, ready to take aim at whatever stirred.

Neither Ben nor I had moved. Slow reflexes, I guess. Then the little doggy door wavered again and everybody froze in position. That's when a little gray and white kitten curiously peered out the doggy door and queried as to what we were doing there. It was like sticking a big balloon with a pin. All the air went out of our crouched stances. Neither of the two reputed big dogs could have gotten more than a nose through that small door but so what? Cops don't get paid to do dogs. Dogcatchers do.

That's when Ben and I went inside armed only with our come-a-longs drawn and cocked, so to speak. They were about as much personal protection as soap on a rope. So we went inside with soap-on-a-rope while a whole bunch of guys stayed outside armed with drawn cannons at the ready.

Ben chased one dog to the left of the walk-around wall separating the kitchen from the living room and I chased the other one around to the right of the same wall. The dogs nodded to each other in passing. After a couple of passes, the dogs got confused and surrendered in disgust. They did bother to bare a fang in a final gesture of defiance before giving up. After all, what is a good guard dog supposed to do when all is lost? They yielded with dignity intact and Ben and I escorted them outside.

Sarge snapped to attention and leveled his rifle in the general direction of the dogs, just in case. 'In case' wasn't needed and we soon had the dogs securely confined in the van's cages. They had already started to like us but we had to put them in cages anyway. If nothing else, it protected them from harm if things went wrong.

Ben and I went back inside just to make sure that there were no more dangerous animals there other than the subject of the whole operation. After all, there could have been a maniacal canary or something.

The officers waved us aside as they prepared to advance down the hallway, implying that we could get hurt. I felt that this was a bit strange at the time because, obviously, we had just spent a considerable amount of time in the home, alone, without guns or support. Our friends with the cannons stayed outside during this phase of the operation and now, all of a sudden, we needed protection?

The officers fell into the standard routine for checking out the situation. One officer covered while another officer advanced with his back against the wall, walking like a crab, sideways, to the first door or opening. The officer then dropped into a crouch while pivoting into the doorway, fanning his weapon around the room.

The second officer also moved in so as to be in a position to back up the first one. Ben and I started to saunter down the hallway but we were waved back out of the line of fire. One of the officers pointed silently to a closed door at the end of the hallway. We would have been directly in front of it if anybody were on the other side of that door. It seemed to us that we had already been exposed to that door but heck, our part of the show was over so we stayed out of the way.

Soon there was only one room left to explore, behind one door. That door, was the closed door down at the end of the hallway. This was the moment of truth. The 9-1-1 caller had to be in there, unless, of course, he had gone out for groceries before we got there.

He had not. The officers burst through the door and a cacophony erupted. There were harsh commands.

"Get down on the floor!" "Put those hands behind your head!" "Sit up!" "Sit down!" "Get out of there!" I couldn't keep track of all the stuff that was going on and I didn't have a big gun pointed at me. It's a wonder the guy didn't do something really normal and get blown away.

Ben and I could not restrain ourselves any longer. We just had to see what was going on. So, braving the non-flying bullets we went down the hallway and into the room to find the poor suspect was totally out of it.

He had withdrawn, wild-eyed and blank-faced into a fetal position and was, I would guess, pretty near catatonic. He was curled up in the bathtub dressed only in shorts. The tub was dry so he wasn't bathing and was probably just hiding there. In his shorts. Bonkers. He had to be institutionalized and it was sad that it turned out that way but it was, overall, an interesting experience.

We did get word later on that he made a complete recovery and was able to reclaim both his life and his dogs.

Another cloud. Another silver lining.

"I've got it. It says, 'cat food, a jug of wine and a pound of henna'."

THE GREAT BASIN WILDLIFE CENTER

A desert is more than just a big sandpile. The Great Basin is a large desert region in the western United States encompassing all of Nevada, nearly a quarter of Utah and small parts of Oregon and California.

 **A BASIN DEVELOPS** when all the ascribed waters evaporate within it. The Great Basin is largely encircled by mountains and therein lies a huge diversity of warm-blooded, as well as cold-blooded creatures. Some view this region as inhospitable. And in part, this is true. But to the animals represented there, it is definitely Home Sweet Home. Another name for home is Ecosystem.

An additional description of an ecosystem is contained in the word 'balance.' Balance is an arrangement where one set of elements equals another. In nature, certain events can tip that scale. Every creature, be it bobcat or pocket mouse, flourishes or wanes, dependent on climate, the availability of food and the abundance of predators. So goes the balance.

Unfortunately, all too often we fail to appreciate this balance and in our ignorance, upset it with disastrous results. Animals once common to the area are now extinct or rare. To know this balance is to respect it. To respect it is to see its populace, not as a mere spectator but as an active participant. We are all very much a part of this vast system, a very demanding and draining part, which entails therefore a great amount of responsibility.

Part of that process is education. Thus the intent of the proposed Great Basin Wildlife Center was to provide some of that education.

The Great Basin Wildlife Center was in effect, to be a mini zoo featuring only exhibits of flora and fauna native to the Basin. Additional exhibits of a historical nature were planned but never quite completed.

These included an Indian village setting illustrating the Shoshone tribe at work and play. A mining display was also to show one of Nevada's principal industries and its most significant one in historical context. Anyway, those projects also never quite made it into reality, together with an anticipated number of species of both plants and animals.

It all started with Dr. Don Hittenmiller who operated the Carson Tahoe Veterinary Hospital. It seems that the good Doctor Don acquired—translation 'got stuck with'—Athena, a superb specimen of *felis concolor*, also known as a mountain lion, puma or cougar.

That lovely lady had been born and raised in captivity on a lion farm somewhere in the east. She was quite tame, very gentle and affectionate but was faced with the prospect of being put to sleep for lack of an appropriate, and legal, home. So Don talked to our Director.

That's when it was decided, quite correctly, that it would be a tragedy for Athena to be destroyed. It was reasoned, again correctly, that a government entity, such as a dog compound, should have little difficulty in jumping the legal hurdles required to obtain and keep a wild animal such as a mountain lion. Never mind that she was more tame than most alley cats. She still had the capabilities of the real thing and was so categorized.

So a new home was built for her next to the Shelter with a wire floor beneath the ground and a roof of wire overhead plus a doublegated entry. It worked great and the public simply loved it.

Not too long after setting up Athena, we happened upon a tame raccoon that the Utah Department of Fish and Game was looking for because he had been unlawfully removed from that state. Its owner had failed to comply with Utah law and continued to violate both Utah and Nevada laws while in our area. So we had to keep him. We added him to our animal collection.

And it seems it never rains but what it pours. While we were in the process of building a coon habitat, we had another problem with the bandit clan. It seems that a certain raccoon couple felt that the redwood deck of a home just up the street would make a neat den and nursery.

Within a matter of days we had box-trapped both parents and all three kids. We hustled in construction of the habitat and all of a sudden we had foreign critters on our hands and a whole lot to learn about them in a heck of a hurry.

So we called in the experts and learned what we needed to know. Five raccoons was a bit too much to handle in captivity so we found new homes for the parents in the wilderness where they belonged. By that time the kids were tame and although, in retrospect, we should have released them into the wild also, we did not. So we had the start of something new. Carson City had nothing else like it.

As for the pouring rain, a typhoon hit. A friend, a comrade in arms, said he knew where there was a tame bear that needed a new home and that if one were not found soon, it too might face euthanasia. I scoffed, convinced that there was no such bear around our area. That's when my friend proved me wrong.

And so our establishment acquired Teddy. What else would you call a bear? A brand new bear cage was donated by a local fence company and Ted had a new place. Would you believe that he had been living at a private residence in Reno for several years? And scarcely anyone knew about it.

That's when our supervisor made a decision that was the best of his career and the worst. He decided that Carson City was mature enough to have a zoo. And the word went out that we would rescue animals that were indigenous to the Great Basin for we were going to name the new zoo the Great Basin Wildlife Center.

With the exception of the raccoons, all of the recent inhabitants of the Center would be nonreturnable to the wild since none had a prayer of a chance for survival on their own due to a number of factors such as over-socialization, lack of necessary survival skills, a shortage of parental natural training or incurred injuries. And so the Great Basin Wildlife Center was born.

In the early days of the Great Basin adventure, we had received a phone call about a wandering coyote but we had pretty much discounted it as a matter of concern. The area in which he was reportedly cruising was not that far away from his normal range.

The next call put him smack dab in the middle of a residential area. Carson sits in the middle of the desert, so any home that is on the fringe of the city is also on the fringe of habitat areas. It is therefore not too unusual to see some form of wildlife coming close to these populated zones. Generally though, they do not come too far into town since they perceive too many man-scents for comfort, hence they instinctively shy away from close, sustained contact. This one was an exception.

His very prolonged presence indicated that something was amiss. The coyote was possibly sick or disoriented, maybe due to injury or worse, due to rabies infection. Something was responsible for the deviation from his normally cautious behavior, as he usually would not be seen in broad daylight in the middle of a populated center.

Before going after him, I loaded the tranquilizer gun, just in case we got close enough to use it safely. It took only a few minutes to arrive in the neighborhood where he had last been seen. My partner and I drove slowly up and down and around the area and soon enough we spotted him. He was not at first aware of us and we decided to sit back and observe for a few moments before closing in.

He stood quite still in the front yard of a home located midblock. Even at that distance he seemed to be abnormal, sort of dazed or confused. He should have been not only exceptionally alert but in motion, seeking a way out, away from the hated and feared smell of man. Instead, he just stood there, both head and tail hung low, drooping. He was obviously not in full command.

As we moved slowly closer, he sensed our approach and moved off in a trot-like gait. But it was not the fluid and graceful motion one might expect. As he moved, we could notice an occasional stagger in which his hind quarters would limp off to one side. His driving rear legs threatened to outrun his front legs and he would assume a U-curve and run a little sideways for a few steps before straightening out. I was becoming certain that we had a rabid coyote on our hands. If so, we could not afford to lose him.

We decided to rush him, to cause him to panic and take off at full speed. We hoped to run him, to tire him, to wear him down and if we were successful in keeping him in sight, to capture him when exhaustion set in.

Naturally, we used the vehicle for this pursuit. I've never met anyone who could physically outrun a fleeing coyote. We stayed close behind him for several blocks as he dashed first up one street then down another.

Finally, he entered a yard that was partially fenced. I grabbed a come-a-long pole and took off after him on foot, hoping to corner him in the fenced area along one side of the house. My partner backed me up with a second catch pole and we worked him around the side of the dwelling toward the rear fence.

Suddenly, realizing that he would soon be trapped, he made a dash for freedom and passed within scant feet of me. My wild lunge almost worked but the noose slipped just over the top of his head and he spurted on by me.

My partner was working to my left and the coyote's right-end run denied him even a chance to capture.

Back again in the vehicle, we continued the pursuit. It began to look as though this coyote didn't know the meaning of the word exhaustion. He would stay just ahead of us, alternately using an energy-saving trot with furious full speed spurts. It was exactly what the military uses for long forced marches: run awhile, walk awhile. It's a very effective way to cover a lot of ground while conserving the maximum amount of energy.

Finally he worked his way out of the developed area and stood at the edge of the desert. He paused there a moment, perhaps to collect his bearings.

Reaching hurriedly for the tranquilizer gun and steadying it on the sill of the open door, I snapped off a quick shot. The dart took him full on the hip. It was a textbook shot, striking the quarry in a well-muscled area and at as near a right angle as possible. Such shots are part skill, part luck.

The dart was purposely overloaded and should have dropped him within seconds. But as the dart struck home, the coyote bolted for the safety of the desert.

I jumped out of the truck, come-a-long in hand, and took off in pursuit. The chase would be short, maybe 50 to 75 yards, before the tranquilizer took effect and dropped him.

Well, so much for best-laid plans of mice and men. What should have happened and what did happen were two different things. First of all, I am not, repeat, not a world-class runner. Given a fair head start I can probably outrun a three-legged obese field mouse, but a coyote is simply out of the question. Not even one as bad off as this one.

He just kept on truckin' toward the horizon, tranquilizer serum bedamned. Not knowing any better and thinking that he couldn't keep it up, I kept it up and stayed on his trail. Just a few more yards and he would have to drop. Fortunately, his pace was a long way from brisk and he stopped every so often to catch his breath or to check my progress. I wasn't sure which it was. I was only grateful for the respite.

We covered a good three-quarters of a mile, maybe more. The last third of it was up a gradually rising hill, although to me it seemed like a vertical cliff.

Finally, he stopped and stood his ground just inside a low fence on a newly built desert home. Cleverly, I made no move toward him, giving him a chance to feel less threatened. Actually, I couldn't move. My vision was blurred, my knees wobbled and my side ached like some hooligan had been thumping on me. It was a question of who would recover first. If the coyote did, he was home free. I was simply finished, burned out, crashlanded. There was no pursuit left in me.

We engaged in a Mexican standoff, glaring balefully at each other for several drawn-out minutes. Eventually a little spark of energy from somewhere deep inside me rose to the surface.

Gingerly, cautiously, I inched closer to him and at last was able to encircle his neck with the loop on the come-a-long. He did not resist for he too was finished.

The occupants of the new house had been watching the final moments of the capture and had telephoned the office to inquire about it. So, my partner had been told of our whereabouts and in a few minutes, he arrived with a van. We loaded Mr. Coyote on board and took him back to the kennel.

We kept him for three days in a spacious but secure quarantine cage, away from people. He made no effort to attack when we entered his cage for feeding. He simply retreated to the farthest corner and watched unblinkingly until we left. He ate well but his condition did not improve in spite of the heavy dose of broad spectrum antibiotics we laced in his food. It was obvious that recovery and release were not in the cards and so we put him to sleep.

His test came back negative for rabies but also failed to show any positives for other diseases. However it had been a chance we could not risk. The wily coyote would not become a part of the new coyote pack already in the Great Basin Zoo.

Also in the early days of the Basin adventure, it became necessary to vaccinate and otherwise treat the animals there, for they were the ones capable of carrying the dreaded rabies virus. It simply would not do for someone to be accidentally exposed to that disease, hence were originated all those signs reading "Keep your hands away from the animals" and "Do not stick your fingers into the cages." Such warnings are absolutely meaningless to children and parents alike.

These inoculations had to be administered by qualified veterinarians and we had one of the best in our volunteer staff. He naturally required some assistance in both capturing the critters as well as holding them still while shots were administered. Any idea who was honored to perform the capture and hold routine?

In the process I relied on the lore that says getting a horse's attention somewhere else before sticking him in the rear end with a hypo needle will deter his attention sufficiently so that he will not associate the ouch with you. There are even some pincer type instruments for this purpose, the name of which escapes me now. Nevertheless, affixing one such to a horse's nose during a shot will supposedly fool him sufficiently so that he won't hold it against you when you stick a needle in his butt. Take my word for it, the wary coyote in our little zoo wasn't so easily fooled.

We had three of them at the Center. Sammy was a pussycat and Wilette was a shy lady who was originally going to be Wile E. Coyote until it was discovered that name did not fit the sex so she became Wilette instead. The latter two were either very forgiving or forgetful for they never held anything against me.

But Cody? Hah! Cody was the alpha male, patriarch of the pack and he never forgot or forgave.

I did not understand Cody's thought processes, and there were no good coyote psychologists around to consult on the subject. Most everything we know about animals is learned from observation or personal experience and we have a tendency afterward to ascribe human motivations and thought patterns to what we have observed.

I would hesitate to delineate Cody's reactions to his zoo surroundings but among them were patience, reticence, caution, fear, instinct, and distrust. Let the others be fooled by socialization. Not Cody.

Just let the man, namely me, approach Cody and there was no question as to who was boss. Head tilted, drool appearing and fire in his eyes, back curved upward like a drawn bow, pawing the ground in mock fury, tail arching, the challenge was clear. He hadn't forgiven me for subjecting him to a rabies shot.

His actions sent a message that said a number of things not spoken. He did not like me. He was afraid but not intimidated, that is to say that he experienced fear in an animal way so his innate defensive postures came into play. He did not attempt to flee and that showed that he was not frightened off. He was willing, albeit reluctantly, to stand his ground.

If others of the pack were present and the threat was near, he always advanced to the front where the pack could best be defended. He also scolded them with throaty growls and if needed, with viciously delivered painful nips. He demanded support in and for his aggressive reactions. In a pack setting, unity of purpose and action are essential for survival and Cody exacted compliance. That is the way of the pack and the pack is stronger for it. In humans, we call it team work.

All three of the coyotes were sociable to other humans to some degree. Sammy was downright friendly and doglike and she especially enjoyed the female members of the staff.

Wilette was a bit standoffish with everyone more or less impartially. She tended to be overly shy but was docile when cornered.

Cody was openly affectionate to some, simply gracious to others and deliberately hostile to me. I was forbidden to the habitat by Cody who would arouse the pack mentality to drive me out. He would coach the pack to circle and make short darting attacks from both front and side while Cody circled to the rear for the real assault. It was easy to see how smaller animals fall prey to the pack and become lunch. When the pack is driven by hunger, it can and will bring down game much larger than themselves.

Cody continued to put on quite a show when I was around. The purpose of the Center was to educate but we did not put on the Cody show for the public. It happened only when it was incidental to some other activity.

However, if there happened to be a crowd present in the habitat when I came upon the scene, it was quite a learning experience for them. It clearly illustrated that wild animals are not pets, no matter how cute they may be. Wild animals are wild animals, Period. When they recognize the need to revert, they do so without warning. They act *now* and it matters not one whit that any human who tries to analyze and explain the reaction cannot figure out the provocation that inspired it. The animal knows and that is enough.

Coyotes are of the order of carnivores and of the specie *Canis Latrans*. In other words, the coyote is a wolflike mammal most closely aligned to the dog. But he is not a dog. As a member of the wolf family, he resembles a poor man's German Shepherd whose growth has been severely stunted and who wears a scraggly hand-me-down coat most of the time except when the hunt is good. Then he's neat and sleek.

The coyote is a native of the Western Plains and has been around at least as long as sheep. Sheepherders think so. He dines on small mammals such as field mice, ground squirrels and rabbits. During lambing season he will go after the newborns.

The coyote is a good stalker and is also a patient hunter who will sit beside a rat hole for hours waiting for the careless occupant to peek outside—for the last time. He will also hunt in packs and will behave in much the same manner as do wolves, circling prey and attacking in quick sprints toward the unprotected flanks. The end is inevitable, only the time is uncertain. Finally, he is cautious around humans and is not normally observed during the middle of the day. Thus the coyotes attracted a lot of attention both from our staff and the public.

As mentioned, all of our guests were native to the Great Basin and most actually dwelled within the boundaries of the state of Nevada. Therefore, we did not have a collection of rare or exotic critters from around the globe. This had been home town stuff on display.

In retrospect, my favorite was Athena, and even though we renamed her Comet as a result of a "Name the Cougar" contest in the local schools, to me she remained Athena. The contest was designed, of course, to promote the Center and to interest the schools in the area to include the Center as a part of the learning experience. Comet was chosen as her name because, in the words of the winning student, "She runs fast and she comes out at night." Nevertheless, that beautiful mountain lion will always top my list.

Theodore, more commonly known as Teddy, was probably our next most popular guest. He was a big black roly-poly bear who loved apples to the point where he had established an apple-eating ritual.

To properly eat an apple, according to Teddy, it was necessary to first lie down. Not just plop down. It was an art form. Recline, first lowering the front end down to knees while bending the rear legs but keeping the big butt up in the air.

Next position the apple between paws. Now lower the posterior down, being careful not to lean to either side. Stay in a vertical mode. Now roll the head to one side and put exactly half of the apple carefully into mouth, using only the side of one paw. No front teeth allowed. Biting down on the apple held in this position, would split it neatly in half. Eat the half which stayed in the mouth and then, when that is devoured, eat the remainder.

Teddy had a favorite log which he played with every day. Two of us buckled our knees just carrying it into the habitat. He merely tossed it around like it was a matchstick. Teddy was not unlike Gentle Ben of TV fame.

Perhaps the most unusual of our zoo friends was Kingman, an American Antelope, sometimes known as a pronghorn. He was neat because he was relatively rare but more so because he had a sweet personality. He seemed to like people. The antelope, incidentally, is Nevada's most fleet-footed of its wildlife.

By law, guest registers are required to be kept on all of our animals but I don't recall the real names of that comical pair of Banditti raccoons that everybody adored. That's because I had unofficially dubbed them Stan and Ollie due to their entertaining antics. They were the compleat clowns even when they weren't trying to be. They would climb and swing from their rafters like a couple of monkeys but their keen intellect told otherwise. They weren't monkeying around.

One of our regular visitors had prepared a rice and venison dish according to a recipe one of his hunting buds had given him. It was awful and a total waste of good rice but Stan and Ollie were of a different mind. They actually liked it, even though they had to relearn an instinctive habit in order to enjoy it.

When we built the coon house we put in a coon pond. And, as raccoons are prone to do, Stan and Ollie dipped their food in the pond. They loved grapes and would wash and eat them as long as you tossed them in their direction. Kid visitors used to enjoy pitching grapes up on the roof of their habitat so the raccoons could scamper up and get them.

But rice cakes were another matter. Every time they tried to wash them, they disintegrated. They did a scrub and rinse routine but when they raised their little hands out of the water, there was nothing there. The look of bafflement was both sad and amusing. However, the bright little critters soon figured out that this particular food had to be eaten without being washed. So, in a very short time they skipped the wash cycle when consuming rice cakes.

Then there was the Opossum pair that we had as guests in our zoo. The possum, as it is commonly known, is a marsupial, which simply means that they have a pouch for carrying their young. They also have given their name to the practice of playing dead to avoid danger from others. Actually, the possum is not play-acting for they are said to actually suffer a temporary paralysis when frightened.

The possum is a grossly unattractive animal and just about as entertaining as watching grass grow. We had a pair of them that could have done double-duty as bookends.

Foxey Loxey needs no further explanation except to say that watching this quick little fox in action explains all of the comments made about his moxie. Being cute as a button doesn't hurt either.

Jingles, the bobcat, provided hundreds of people with the opportunity for a close-up look at this fascinating but elusive feline. Not at all timid, Jingles primped and preened for the public with unabashed admiration for himself. He permitted handling on his terms and one had always to be alert to observe the signs which said enough is enough. It was not advisable to go beyond Jingles' open mouth and hiss stage. Other than that, Jingles was a love but don't mess with his chow. That was always forbidden fruit, even if you had just delivered it to him personally.

For a time we had a petting zoo for the little ones, complete with George the turkey, plus some sheep and goats. Most of the little kids and sometimes a parent or two spent considerable time indulging both themselves and the petees.

In the feathered realm, we had a lovely red-tailed hawk and a turkey vulture. But best of all, we had two golden eagles.

The golden is one of the most majestic of birds and has an awesome wingspread and huge talons. Ours were not capable of sustained flight and could not be released in the wild, but they were certainly awesome in captivity.

Rescue and Pledge were just a tad faster in movement than the possum but were nevertheless a big hit. They were desert tortoises recovered from the Las Vegas developers' shovels. The western tortoise is on the endangered list, hence is carefully pampered in Nevada.

We also had at the zoo a land shark in deer's clothing. There were times when he could be especially nice and this often involved the presence of children. But he was not so delightful around adults. He was often downright objectionable in spite of the fact that we called him Bambi. Maybe that was what did it. He hated his name.

The Center, unfortunately, although well received, was short-lived, for various reasons. Nothing is forever. In the case of the Great Basin Wildlife Center, we who worked to create it also had to work to let it go. The Center was closed due to a number of factors beyond our control.

All of our delightful guests went to new homes in private zoos. Maybe we were not destined to have a Center yet. Perhaps the City was not big enough to support one. Perhaps some other time will see the Center, or something similar, come back to life. Who knows? Maybe it was for the best. But I'll bet that in years to come, some kid turned adult will look back and remember various truly memorable moments spent at the Great Basin Wildlife Center!

It was a remarkable project.

The telephone rang at 5:30 in the morning. God himself doesn't get up until six o'clock after his assistants have properly placed the sun in its daily orbit. No self-respecting human would voluntarily get up that early excepting in dire emergency. And dogcatchers seem to inherit dire emergencies.

THE CLANGING BELL presaged a crisis of some sort. It is the scourge of the catcher's world: *dispatch*, no doubt announcing some animal-related catastrophe. And it was. It seems some scroungy little terrier type had sniffed once too often at the hole his master had dug in order to erect a concrete-based post. Hence a large posthole.

Little Scruffy apparently slipped and gravity did the rest. Down into the hole he went. He not only had the audacity to be a klutz, he was also indecent enough to put on the old helpless act. His owners responded to his plaintive yelps and called us to do the rescue bit.

Some of those little dogs are such terrible whiners they equate every misstep with Armageddon. Actually, the trap in which Scruffy found himself was just a muddy hole in the ground. But his wails had elicited such attention he managed to get everybody in the neighborhood involved, which in turn caused me to get up at 5:30.

By the time I arrived he had already extricated himself from the oozing mess and was having breakfast. They probably slaughtered the fatted calf for him and I hadn't even had coffee yet. Such is a dogcatcher's life.

BUT THE CATCHER'S THIRD EYE must be keen, adept at perceiving things unseen, sharp enough to spot that invisible railroad that runs right down the middle of Carson's main thoroughfare. There are no trains on it. What matters is that it establishes a great divide, the one that separates the privileged from the rest of us. It's that symbolic railway, the track that signifies whether you were born on its right or wrong side.

Sometimes the track runs down one street, sometimes another. In Carson, the line divides the east from the west, the west being the plum locale. Within the west side lies the Historic District, site of many of the grander old homes of yesteryear. They once housed the Ferris Wheel's inventor and such Comstock figures as one Samuel Clemens. The gracious Governor's Mansion heads the list.

But all of the West Side history is not in the dim past. Something really significant to film buffs happened there just a few short years ago. The late great John Wayne slept there! He was making the movie *The Shootist*, his last film. It featured the old Krebb-Peterson house on Mountain Street, just a few homes away from the Governor's mansion. The film included Lauren Bacall, Ron Howard and a small part for somebody named Jimmy Stewart. It had to be a success with that cast.

The movie was typical Western Wayne at his best in which he played an aging gunfighter who was terminally ill. His character was that of an irascible but thoroughly lovable gent in spite of his profession. By the advent of his demise in the movie, viewers had become enamored of him and the strength of his character. It was a sad ending and the home today emits some of that sadness as tourists pass by.

That was particularly true last week. A young doe attempted to clear the wrought iron fence around the house to browse on the tender bushes within. A miscalculation figured in. Dew probably caused a slippery takeoff and she became painfully impaled on the spiked fence. She was so severely injured we couldn't save her. She was only in search of a rose.

ON THE SAME SIDE OF THE TRACKS was another old mansion featuring a weathervane. Those ornaments were an art form for early blacksmiths. They adorned the exposed peaks and ridges of homes and barns and sometimes just wound up atop a tall pole. Their north arrows pointed out the direction of windflow while the south pointer showed from whence it had come.

Quite often the vane had little appendages showing the east and west of things but it didn't really matter anyway. They were just there, a status symbol. They became collector's items.

But the most recent weathervane on Crain Street was none of the foregoing. It was a dog and, unlike its predecessors, did not point out wind directions.

But he did do an OK job of pointing. He pointed out the mailman, the newspaper boy and where the guy with the big dog had gone. And he punctuated his point with a bark or two, just so passersby understood his mission.

The first time I heard about the wacky vane I presumed I was going to a rescue. Dogs on roofs usually need rescuing. That logic was faulty. This vane just liked it up there. It gave him a different view of the world, such as what it was like to be as tall as a basketball star.

We soon discovered that he could attain this vantage point by going up the stairway to a choice bedroom and then availing himself of an open unscreened window. *Voila!* Instant perspective!

But it took a month of Sundays to quiet the phone calls and convince neighbors that the doggy weathervane only had a behavioral problem and didn't need to be saved from his folly.

ONE OF THOSE DAYS

Today was one of those days. You know what that means. We've all had to contend with those days.

ACTUALLY, it started out the day before yesterday and sort of worked its way forward. My left foot and my right wrist are just beginning to feel normal again.

It was two days ago when one of the guys who works in the factory across the street came into the office and with a perfectly straight face announced that one of the dogs in our kennel had escaped. That meant panic time. We have one of those thirty-five mile an hour speed limit streets in front of the kennel on which everybody does sixty. So naturally, I was alarmed.

We don't own the dogs in our kennel. We only have temporary custody. It is therefore with double anxiety that we face the loss of any animal: First, we do not want to lose one of our charges. Period. And second, we may have to account to an owner for the loss. I mean, how do you tell somebody who comes in to reclaim his pet that we 'seem to have lost him,' hence my alarm.

I readied myself for a dash out into the street when the gent said, "Not to worry. The dog is up on the roof and until he gets down, he is quite safe."

Somewhat mollified by the knowledge that the dog was not going to be run down by a speeding eighteen-wheeler, but equally mystified by the news that he was roof-bound, I went outside to see for myself.

Frankly, I was more than a bit skeptical. I mean, I know how the kennel is built and there is just no way that a dog could be up on the roof unless I had put him there, which I hadn't.

So much for healthy skepticism. She, not he, it turned out, was indeed there, pacing back and forth and wondering what kind of mess she had gotten herself into this time.

It was time to play detective and figure out how she had gotten up there. I went back inside and put on my Columbo raincoat, sans cigar. I was then able to reconstruct the probable events which led to there being a Siberian Husky on the roof of the Shelter.

Each of the two gates to the dog run were latched and locked and she didn't have a key. But she had apparently shinnied up the front gate, which is located on an outdoor segment of the run, until she made it to the top. She then inserted herself between the top of the gate and the run's mesh cover while simultaneously rolling over on her back. While thus hanging half in and half out of the enclosure, she had wiggle-squirmed up and onto the chain link top of the pen.

Yes, I know. It can't be done, at least not by a dog. But she did it anyway. Once that far, it was an easy jump to the roof and that is where I found her. She did a much better job of it than I did. I slipped off almost before I got started and that is where the wrist-foot business happened.

My second attempt was much improved over the first and she was soon back where she belonged, except in a tighter run. The rest of yesterday was more of the same only different and that brings us all the way to today.

And it is still one of those days that never go right. The next matter at hand was something out of the ordinary. It seems that those pesky Mustangs had once again strayed off of their range and were down at the edge of town munching the hay that belonged to their more domesticated brethren that dwell in the assorted pastures and corrals dotting the outskirts.

Mustangs are wild horses and wild horses are properly the province of the Bureau of Land Management, BLM to those who love the alphabet soup of government agencies. However, since the BLM wardens are few and far between, we often respond to their calls. We don't do anything heroic or even cowboyish. We just chase the Mustangs back up into the hills from whence they came and to whence they belong.

Now, a horse is pretty big. Right? Weighs about eight hundred pounds or so? Stands about five or six feet tall eye-to-eye? Should be pretty easy for an old pro to spot, wouldn't you think? Especially if there are eight or ten of them running around the neighborhood.

But after better than half an hour of driving the bumpy trails and walking the sagebrush, I hadn't spotted a single one. All I got for my trouble was a little more gimp in my left foot and two socks full of assorted foxtails and other prickly stuff. Meanwhile, other calls were backing up and crying for attention.

Among them, I took a report on a cat that was shot with a BB or pellet gun. The wound was fortunately superficial and I promised a follow-up investigation.

Elsewhere, another cat, overcome with curiosity, had done some investigating of her own and wedged herself into a fireplace insert. I attempted to cajole, entice and otherwise pull her out but just wound up with a face full of soot for my efforts.

I assured the owners that since she was not actually trapped, just recalcitrant, she would no doubt extricate herself in her own good time. Just leave her alone to do it.

"Fine," they said, but gave the distinct impression they weren't convinced.

But by the time I got back to the Center for a face wash and clean clothes, they had called to report success. Thank you very much. Soot isn't easily cleaned from shirt collars.

Next, it was time to coax the truck five miles up the side of a canyon on the worst excuse for a dirt road extant. There were two ranches on a plateau at the top and it seems that a combination Rottweiler-Great-Dane-Moose fell madly in love with the sheep-herder's Queensland. Said swain was so enamored of his fair lady that he was an easy catch, although he was a bit heavy for loading into the truck.

The road back down hadn't gotten any better since I went up but the Big Guy and I finally made it to the bottom without mishap. The only bright spot was a good sized buck deer and his mate which graced the scenery briefly. That's always a welcome sight and one of the benefits of sparse human population.

Down at ground level, another call. More Mustangs. You guessed it. Once again, I could not find a single one of them. They just seemed to disappear the minute I showed up. So much for that effort.

But it wasn't over yet. Our Department does not have sufficient staff to operate on an around-the-clock basis. Most cities cannot afford that luxury either.

But emergencies do happen. And such incidents, like ladies having babies, almost always occur at the most inopportune times. It's some kind of natural law at work. I think it's God's way of keeping us on our toes.

In order to respond to those off-the-wall events, someone on staff is always designated to do standby duty. Standby means don't leave town. Be available to a phone. Wear a pager everywhere and the shower is no exception. Nowadays, we can carry a cell phone, but the pager is usually mandatory since it is not subject to being out of range.

Some pagers beep. Others chirp, tweetle, vibrate or squeal. Ours is an indiscreet wailing sound something like British Constables' patrol cars, only more shrill, and thankfully, of shorter duration.

In the event of any emergency, the pager does its beep thing and the duty officer responds. Our pagers are audio as well and so the caller usually follows with a brief message such as, "Call the dispatcher." Their demeanor is professional and serious as befits the nature of the call.

But this time it was different. I could discern a suppressed chuckle in her voice when I responded by telephone to the pager's beep. She requested that I meet with two officers from the Sheriff's Office in the parking lot fronting the Department of Motor Vehicles. There was just a hint of a snicker there. And then a pregnant pause.

I guessed that it was my turn to play straight man like in a Burns and Allen routine. So, following the pause, in the best tradition of the theater, I fed her the next line.

"What is the problem that these officers need my assistance?"

"The swing shift clerk wants to go home," she said. Then she let it lie.

Time for a straight line again.

"So, OK. Why doesn't she do that?"

"The dog won't let her," was the response, as though that cleared it all up for me. Why hadn't I discerned that before?

I could see that we were rapidly getting nowhere and I could feel old age creeping up on me if we kept this up so, dispensing with the one-liners, I got to the point. And the situation began to take shape.

It seems that when the clerk got off duty at 10:00 p.m., she found, much to her dismay, a Shepherd in her unlocked, open windowed Volkswagen Bug. Not feeling too comfortable about opening a door with this strange dog sitting in it, she had called the Sheriff for help.

The two officers who responded to the scene didn't feel any too gung-ho about it either. It seems that this was the biggest German Shepherd any of them had ever seen. Up close and personal, he was formidable. He filled the entire front seat of the Bug. And even though such front seat isn't too big, it still takes a big hunk of dog to fill one.

It was dark in the parking lot and even with flashlights, it wasn't possible for the officers to judge the temper of this canine. In short, nobody wanted to open the door and inquire if Rover would like to come out and play. Neither officer wanted to shoot first and ask questions later so they called for assistance.

When I got there I could see why they were hesitant. This was one big dog, classic German Shepherd. Pride in his lineage literally emanated from him as he sat there radiating the impression that he had every right to be there and showed a willingness to contest the point with anyone who had a mind to do so. A most impressive canine.

I figured such a masterful animal must have had some training. At least I was willing to gamble on it. So, with everybody standing way back, I opened the car door and in my best First Sergeant voice ordered the dog out and down. Bingo! It worked. He came out and immediately went into the classic 'down' position. After that it was a simple matter to put a leash on him and escort him into the van.

While this little scenario was being played out, the lady and the two officers stood by incredulously, wide-eyed, open-mouthed. It did look awesome.

Really, it was not. After a while, we doggy people get pretty experienced at reading dogs. It comes after passing Capture 101 and Advanced Capture 201 at the School of Hard Knocks. Usually you can tell when a dog is vicious, a fear biter or just normally defensive. There are signs. The obvious ones include raised hackles or tucked tails and are fairly easy to see and readily explainable.

There are others that you cannot explain. You just know when a dog cannot be handled or when it is all bluff. It is that thing called experience. You learn it by doing it. Once in a while you may misinterpret the signs and get bitten. That's a hazard that goes with the territory but it is also a good learning experience as it tends to teach you to look more carefully and read better next time.

Good results are gratifying when handling a situation favorably that might have gone badly. Especially when you have an appreciative audience!

"This little tweed number is guaranteed to match whatever color fur your dog sheds."

TAFFY

Taffy was a trick. Some might even say she was a dirty trick, although I never considered her acquisition as such. I concede that my attitude about the matter might, in some small measure, be attributable to the fact that it was I who was doing the tricking, if trickery there be. If someone else had done it, I might consider it differently. You see, it's all a matter of perspective.

ANYWAY, TAFFY WAS one of those thousands of pets that, for some reason or another, was no longer wanted. She was advertised in the local newspaper's classified section as a 'free to good home' dog. If ever there was a phrase that should raise the hackles, that is it.

How in the world can you know with any degree of certainty that a beloved pet is going to a good home? It's a crap shoot. I guess it is a prime example of what is meant by being between a rock and a hard place. People, faced with a problem requiring that they relinquish a pet, can only hope that they are doing the right thing by giving it away because the alternatives are too distasteful to contemplate.

It was never our intent to acquire a pet for ourselves. But we already had a good home picked out for Taffy if she were suitable. The ad sounded good. We responded without misgivings. The current owners were eager to meet with us and in short order we completed the arrangements to get together for pet show-and-tell.

You see, Grandma and Grandpa both wanted and needed a dog to dote upon and spoil. They shared a fondness for Cocker

Spaniels and wouldn't you just know it, Taffy happened to be one. Their fondness stemmed from a natural love for the breed, reinforced by their adoration of 'Lucky,' a sweet little Cocker they lost to ancient age. So, Taffy seemed like a sure thing, a natural choice to fill the cavity left by Lucky.

When we arrived at the unveiling they told us all about Taffy. She was five years old, sweet of temper, totally housebroken, loved kids and everything that moves and most things that don't. Pure salesmanship, especially the point about being age five. There was not a drop of truth in that one, we found. It was a used car salesman's line relative to the car that only went to church on Sunday, with the little old lady in tennis shoes, from Pasadena. Taffy would never see five again, or even eight or nine. All of her future years would be numbered in double digits. No matter. Taffy seemed to be the perfect pet for the folks. If not, the owners assured us we could return her.

We quickly relearned Pet Lesson Number One. Never, repeat never, choose a pet for someone else. When you do so, you have at best a fifty-fifty chance of its being acceptable. Or, to put it another way, it's even money that your selection will be rejected. It was. It seems that poor old Taffy was too fat, 'way too fat, for Gram to handle.

I did my best to point out that Taffy didn't need to be handled. She was more than capable of jumping up onto the couch or bed by herself. In fact, she probably could have made it to the chandelier if she had reason enough to do so. Then there was the food. She didn't like Gram's choice of dog food.

My arguments were to no avail. Taffy would have to go back to her original owners and gamble on getting a set of new ones. I knew from experience that her chances ranged from slim to none. She was getting rather long in tooth, as the expression goes. Sooner or later, age does us all in and Taffy was well past the halfway point.

Remembering that Taffy's owners had told us that we could return her if things didn't work out, that seemed the only option. We certainly didn't need another dog around the house. Glenna was really quick to point out this fact to me in case I had missed the obvious.

"No, no, no, absolutely not. And that's final!" was her edict.

Being of sound mind and body, at least for the moment, I quickly agreed. The dog had to go, just as soon as I could contact her old owners and make the arrangements. We already had two dogs and two cats. Enough was enough. Still, I kinda liked the fat little critter.

At least twice a day, sometimes thrice, I would attempt to call Taffy's former owners. At least twice a day, sometimes thrice, I would put one little pinky down on the receiver's button and thereby break the connection. Strange to tell, Taffy's former owners never once answered a single one of those calls. Glenna bought the story hook, line and sinker.

After several days of frustrated attempts, I delayed the daily call until quite late one evening. As I got up from my easy chair in front of the TV, I pointed out to my wife the lateness of the hour. The only purpose in doing so was to add an additional little cover to my backside for my previous failures to make contact. I knew that I had played out this little scam about as far as I could. Taffy's time was up, her moment had come. This was really it. The call would go through. Arrangements would be made and Taffy would be returned to her former home tomorrow. No little pinky tricks this time.

I dialed and the phone began to ring. A sudden summons from my wife in the next room and the phone gratefully slammed back into its cradle. She had relented, she said. She changed her mind, she said. We might as well keep Taffy, she said. Too many days had gone by, she declared, reluctantly, and it just was not reasonable to expect the old owners to take her back now.

Soberly I considered her words and agreed that she was probably right. We would keep Taffy.

Until now, the truth has never been told!

SNOOPY

SNOOPY IS A NEUTERED MALE PIT BULL TERRIER. Snoops, as he is affectionately known at the veterinary hospital, belongs to one of those Mr. Macho types who would never, not ever, neuter a male dog. It's indecent to even think of it. The philosophy of the machos is that it is OK to alter a female but males are less real if so subjected to surgery. So how come Snoops is at the vet's getting fixed? Was he broken?

Yes, in a manner of speaking, he was indeed. He got himself rather badly broken when these two guys jumped out of their car and fled on foot when stopped by the police on a routine traffic stop. It was an insignificant stop, a minor offense that usually results in a warning being given or a fix-it ticket being issued. No big deal. No citation. That is, if the culprits had not run away.

But run they did. They ran this way. They ran that way. The officer who stopped them in the first place called for backup and then he too ran. Pretty soon a whole bunch of guys showed up and they too began to run.

Out-gunned and out-run, the two desperados took refuge in a nearby townhouse which happened to belong to a friend and said friend happened to not be at home at the time. He might not have admitted the two fleeing thug types into his home if he had been there. The door was unlocked with Snoopy being the only occupant.

So they took their uninvited selves upstairs, really upstairs, all the way into the attic. They went up through the access hatch in the ceiling of the walk-in closet and once in the crawl space, flipped the hatch cover back into place.

Since the police, under certain circumstances, are authorized to pursue a fugitive into a dwelling without first procuring a search warrant, this situation was deemed by the pursuing officers to be such a time and after only a brief consultation amongst themselves, they entered Snoopy's home in pursuit of the fugitives.

A quick search of the downstairs rooms and closets failed to turn up the fleet-footed ones and it was therefore obvious that the only way left to go was up. So up they went.

The officers ascended the staircase using the approved dash-and-cover technique even though this was a bit difficult to do when going up a closed and narrow stairway.

Then they proceeded in their search of two upstairs bedrooms. In the first room they found no one so they opted to explore the second one. When they opened that door, they were confronted by none other than Snoopy.

Understand that I was not there during that incident so I do not know what happened next. I offer no opinion nor make any judgment of any sort. But I have it on good authority that it was a fearful situation to be faced by a Pit Bull, full of teeth, coming straight at you. I can only assume that Snoopy did just that and the officers reacted.

At any rate, poor old Snoops got shot by the defending officers and one of those shots sort of emasculated him. The veterinary hospital simply finished up the job. They also had to complete a couple of other repairs as well, for Snoops had absorbed three rounds from a 9-millimeter handgun and was a bit damaged, to say the least.

He didn't really seem to be bothered by the whole thing when I picked him up a short time later. Pits are tough.

But I think it should be emphasized at this point that the Carson City Sheriff's Department is made up of one heckuva great bunch of good guys. They have a fund to which they contribute out of their own pockets for special occasions such as when one of their own is injured or has a family problem. It is a small fund and takes a long time to build.

But they voted to use it to fix up poor Snoops because it wasn't his fault that all these strange guys invaded his house and he got the dirty end of it. After all, it *was* his house!

So Snoops got well and the sheriff's department got a bit poorer while the bad guys eventually got what they deserved. 🐾

THE SUBSTITUTE

I like dogs. It must be inborn, something in my nature, because I did nothing to develop it. Some people like dogs in general. Others will tolerate only a specific breed.

CARSON CITY is, in many ways, still a cow town. It seems that newcomers to this area immediately recognize this truth and go out and get a pickup truck with a rifle rack across the rear window and add *two* big dogs to put into the back of the truck. The most common breed in that scenario is the Labrador Retriever. However, a number of other breeds are acceptable for truck-filling. Incidentally, dogs transported in open-bed pickups are, at this writing, legal in Nevada, but not so in some other states.

But for Harry, there was only one dog suitable to fill his pickup—a dog named Murphy. He was relatively small, a Welsh Corgi, in fact.

Murph, as I called him, was Harry's companion and did a great job of keeping Harry on his exercise toes. Harry, well past middle age and severely handicapped, was much less so because of Murphy who forced Harry to get off his butt and man his aluminum crutches to take Murphy outside. Often.

Harry took up oil painting to fill his long hours and Murph was his best critic. Murphy didn't like any of them. The reality was that many of Harry's early efforts were pretty bad. But, like fine wine, the results improved with age. Or maybe it was effort. I have one of his works which he completed after he had been painting for a couple of years and it is commendable. But Murphy continued to criticize and spur Harry on to greater effort.

I first met these two when I happened by the house one sunny day when Murph had taken Harry away from painting for one of their frequent front yard romps. I was so impressed with how neat Murphy was that I had to stop and get acquainted. Our friendship grew from that moment and I stopped whenever I was in the neighborhood and had a few minutes to spare.

Time passed and Murph, Harry and I all got older. Harry started to get a bit forgetful and sometimes would become confused as well. There were a couple of times when he took Murphy to the groomers and then forgot where he had left him. Thinking Murphy was lost, he'd called Animal Control to report Murphy missing. He would usually remember soon after and phone back to apologize for bothering us.

He also started sending Murph to the groomers even though the dog didn't need it and had just been there a week or so before.

Harry's mobility, by that time none too good at best, had also diminished. As a result, he had to sell his truck which had been equipped with hand controls to allow him to operate it without having full use of his legs. That meant that now he had to rely on others to drive him around.

Then one day Murphy just up and died. It was shocking to everyone who knew these two and it was absolutely and totally devastating to Harry.

I don't know if Harry was a religious man, but he must have been doing some tall praying for, one day not too long after Murph crossed over to the other side, something good happened. That something good was a Welsh Corgi and she showed up at the pound, available for adoption.

That was rare for Carson City. Being big dog country, there are not too many spare Corgies around these parts. Somehow, this one never made it to the official 'available for adoption' list. By some mysterious quirk of fate, the only person who got a chance at that critter was Harry and he didn't have much to say in the matter either. I just took the Corgi to Harry and said, "Here's your new dog," and that settled that.

As far as I was concerned, it was a match made in heaven, as though in answer to a prayer. Never mind that this little lady was of a different gender, she soon became Murphy to Harry. He was less able than I had realized but in a remarkably short time he made the mental transfer from the deceased Murphy to the new Murphy. In other words, he completely wiped from his mind the fact that the original Murphy had died and that this was a new dog. Harry would have none of that. Murphy was Murphy, one and the same. I thought that was a helpful situation, but it turns out I was wrong.

It never dawned on me that there would be other people who had a stake in what went on in Harry's life. But there were others. A number of others. And they were the people behind the scenes who cleaned the house, mowed the lawn, did the laundry and such, *ad infinitum.*

Caregivers are the unsung heroes and heroines to people like Harry. Well, I soon heard from the Boss Lady of that group. She was not happy with the new Murphy and felt that I had seriously stuck my nose in where it did not belong. And she was right.

If the new Murph were unwelcome, how and who would explain this to Harry? Who would tell him that the dog had to go? It was hardly fair to pass this heavy burden on to someone else and to make that person the bad guy.

It was equally unfair to burden the caregivers with the care of a dog over which they had no option in its acquisition. So, they rightfully stuck me with the job of telling Harry that the new Murphy was obsolete.

I screamed. How could I do that to Harry? I needed a way out, and quickly. I wound up asking for a reprieve. Let the dog stay for two weeks, I pleaded, on the basis that Harry's well-being would be so improved by the presence of the new Murph that it would offset the care needed for the dog.

Guess what? It worked. And was I ever glad, because I would rather have gone to the dentist without novocaine than to face up to Harry with the news that his dog was a goner.

Actually, I think the truth of the matter was that while Harry did improve during those two weeks, it was everyone else falling in love with the new Murph that carried the tide. Whatever, I was certainly happy that it worked out well and I learned a hard lesson from it.

(But I would do it again!)

RENEGADES

*I met another dog named Thor today. The other
Thor was a German Shepherd and as the work-
ings of coincidence would have it, so was this
one. But there was one huge difference. This Thor
was a girl dog where the original Thor had been
a guy type. Presumption that the name might
have been a nickname would be wrong. It was
just plain Thor.*

THOR'S OWNER is also a lady and she agrees that Thor is a
strange name for a female dog but since it was Thor when she got
it, and the dog likes it, Thor it remained.

She had wandered off by herself one fine morning and was
sauntering through one of the city's nicest mobile home parks
when one of the residents spotted her and called us. The park was
quiet and somewhat secluded, once inside, but it was bordered on
three sides by heavily traveled streets and was not therefore a
good place for a dog to be running loose.

Running would perhaps be too grandiose a term for what
Thor was doing. More appropriately, she was strolling around
and, on occasion, lounging. She did put on a bit of speed now and
then to avoid me as I pursued her on foot but she never raised a
dust cloud or a sweat line on her brow as she persistently walked
around the nearest corner and then waited to see if I would catch
up to her.

The van's radio beckoned me while I was debating the best
way to catch this reluctant lass and the office advised me that the

owner of the dog was, at that moment on the line inquiring about her missing dog. Arrangements were made for me to meet said owner in the park while I kept a wary eye on Thor.

That was fairly easy since Thor had settled in a shady spot and never budged an inch, at least not until her owner arrived. At that point, Thor got up and moved off in the opposite direction. I guess she wasn't finished with her outing yet.

I moved the van to cut off her escape route and her owner called entreaties to her to come on back. After a moment or two, Thor got her faculties all together and decided to go for a ride. She was obviously, not exactly a youngster any more. That's when she suddenly went from not having anything at all to do with me to 'I can't get enough of this guy' and tried her best to board the van via the driver's seat.

However, her advancing age and a touch of arthritis soon convinced her that the van was a bit too high to access. She gave up and went home quite contentedly with her owner. Another satisfactory doggy encounter.

THEN THERE WAS the Priest and the good Shepherd.

I received a call about a dog that was not staying home so I went to investigate. It turned out that this dog was not really the man's dog. It just showed up one day a week or two previously at this guy's house and decided to stay. Stay, that is, in a manner of speaking. The guy allowed the dog to hang around but he did not call us to inform us that the dog was there. We cannot put lost and found dogs together until we hear both sides of the situation. Anyway, the gent had decided to keep the dog so he hadn't bothered to report finding it.

Young Sheps, for all their magnificent features, are really crocodiles in disguise. They rend objects unrecognizable. This dog was no exception and did his fair share in reducing useful objects to rubble.

Plus, he had a couple of other unsavory traits such as having been born on the wrong side of every door.

It seems that young Shep would ask once, softly, to have the sliding door opened for him and if that were not done quickly, he would attempt to dig under the sliding door. That is tough on carpets and subflooring as well.

Once outside for a moment or two, he would repeat the request and, if not readmitted immediately, he would repeat the action and thus ruin the whole decor, inside and out.

He also had a severe hearing impediment as well and absolutely did not hear, or care to respond to anything other than the dinner bell. This selective hearing loss also created in him a learning disability which resulting in incorrigibly bad habits. In effect, he dug his way into doggy jail.

The lost and found log failed to provide an original owner which leads to the conclusion that the original owner did not search too diligently for this lost pet. Given the dog's numerous bad habits, it appeared that he would not be a good candidate for adoption. His striking good looks were his only socially redeeming assets but good looks alone usually do not get the job done.

Then along came the Catholic Priest who was being retired from active duty. It seems that the Archdiocese owned a home way out in the desert in an area which is isolated miles from anywhere. Solitude City. Remote.

There is that highway in Nevada that has earned the title of 'The loneliest road in the world.' The reality is that many, if not most, of the highways in that State deserve such appellation. So the Priest had this house out west of nowhere on one of those lonely roads and needed companionship spelled with a capital C, as in canine.

That's when he decided on a dog and he was partial to Shepherds. We did a rather thorough job of describing Shep's crocodilian habits and chronicled his other shortcomings as well. But the Priest figured he could handle the dog anyway. After all, it would have several square miles in which to run and nary a soul to bother, so why not?

And Father Priest did handle it for quite a while, for several months in fact, but the inside-outside trick finally turned the tide against the dog. The Shep happened to be inside at the time and outside was where he wanted to be. The back porch of the ranch house had been glassed in and screened for both summer and winter enjoyment. The door was equipped with a closer and stayed shut automatically but it did not have a latch. Just push or pull and in or out you go.

That apparently was too complex for young Shep. Crash, tinkle, freedom. Minus one window of course. It is a wonder that the dog did not slash himself to death. Naturally, he was no sooner outside than he decided inside was where he'd rather be, so he returned to the porch.

Was it too logical to think that the dog, having just gone out a window would choose the same route to return? Instead it chose to come in through the door, without bothering to open it. He simply hurled himself through the upper half of it, the half that formerly had screen on it. In less than five minutes he had taken out both a window and a door and in the process assured himself a return to the pound. And return he did.

Normally, this incorrigible conduct would have spelled demise for the dog, training not being an option. It had all been tried before and the effort was a failure from the start. But somehow the final solution was not to be enacted, yet.

Within the first 24 hours of Shep's incarceration at the Shelter, another man came in and spied the Shep which, by that time, was beginning to look pretty impressive as maturity approached. His gangly youth had begun to turn downright aristocratic and he did indeed make a great impression.

Normally, this would not have saved him for good looks alone do not make for suitable adoptions. We are required to make hard choices and this dog had certainly shown that he was not an asset to the community.

His new role in life however, required very little more than just looking good. He was to be a junkyard dog. Surely, he could do no harm there as he only had to hang around and look fierce. Well, he didn't do any harm. He just disappeared.

End of story? Huh-uh. With the dog's destructive demeanor he should have been history. Not so. It did take a couple of more months for Shep to come home to roost but come home he did.

In all, he had been in and out of the pound twice and in private homes three times. So where did he show up next?

He came back to the beginning, back to where it all started, back to the house with the sliding door and the torn carpet.

And somewhere along the way he went to school and earned his Ph.D. and turned himself into a well-trained and obedient dog, without a hearing impediment. He stayed that way for many fruitful years until old age took him to the other side of the Big Door.

"No...he doesn't dig holes in the yard anymore."

SYMBIOSIS

IT IS UNLIKELY that there are many around who do not know of Lassie, perhaps the most famous dog of all times. Lassie appeared first in the movies, then later on in the early days of television and finally in reruns up to and including the present.

I don't mind admitting that Lassie was the hero, dogwise, of my youth, along with the thousands of other kids who sat on seat edges in theaters across the country watching her misadventures.

Lassie was that lovable big Collie dog with a luxurious coat of sable hue. She lived on a farm with a young boy and an adoring family at a time when life was simple and uncomplicated relative to today's standards.

Nevertheless, she managed to get into and out of more trouble than any ten dogs could in as many lifetimes and still survive. Lassie was better at survival than any cat and had many more than the traditional nine lives, a fact which would turn any feline green with envy.

If I remember the episodes correctly, Lassie performed a major miracle in one of them by having a litter of the cutest Collie pups ever born. That was quite a feat for Lass since the experts of the day seemed to agree that Lassie was always played by a male dog!

One of the most outstanding of her many talents was her singular instinct as a four-legged homing pigeon. She always seemed to have the Angel of Divine Guidance sitting on her shoulder for she invariably found her way home from Siberia or the Yucatan Peninsula with equal ease, undaunted by swollen rivers, fierce wolves, deadly rattlesnakes, scorching deserts, treacherous quick-sands, sheer cliffs and truly villainous villains.

No matter the crisis, she wended her way home with unerr-ing accuracy, all I might add, to the delight of movie audiences who wouldn't budge from their seats even for free buttered pop-corn until Lassie was safely back home again.

The Lassie series was based on symbiosis, defined as a rela-tionship existing between two or more unlike organisms in which each derives a beneficial result from that association. Such are not casual relationships, but rather one of survival, a technique of co-operative living. The development of a coral reef is often given as an example of symbiotic relationship.

An even clearer example is that of the termite that is host to a protozoa which lives in its system and derives all of its nourish-ment from the food taken in by the termite. It has no other source from which to obtain food and thus to survive. In so doing, it breaks down the cellulose eaten by the termite in such a way that it becomes the termite's food. Without that protozoa, the cellulose would not nourish the termite and it would die of starvation. Thus, each is wholly dependent on the other for life.

There is a relatively similar mutual relationship between ca-nines and humans, each providing sustenance in various catego-ries which are of invaluable benefit.

Prime examples of similar unions include such as the service dogs that provide a constant flow of love, devotion and assistance to accident victims, those with mobility impairments, or the hear-ing or visually impaired who have suffered permanent disabilities.

They are frequently wheelchair bound or otherwise handi-capped. Rhesus monkeys also serve in this capacity, handling many small chores for paraplegics, thus facilitating their master's daily lives. In those instances the animal gives and in giving also receives. Its master likewise receives and in receiving gives back. Such animals thus bring new hope and inspiration to those who might otherwise be left tragically alone. Such situations are typi-cally the true essence of a symbiotic relationship.

Then there is an interesting couple consisting of a critter and master but forgive me if I give top billing to the critter. The canine in this relationship is named Scout and is a duly certified Deputy Sheriff with the Carson City Sheriff's Department.

Scout wears a badge and receives all the respect that goes with it as she goes about her business. Her business? She's a lean, mean drug sniffin' genius. And while her body says Labrador, her heart says German Shepherd, and when called upon to prove it, she's got more than enough true grit to go around.

As a matter of fact, it took a bit of time and training for Scout to mellow out, for she was a bit too aggressive at first. Now however, she goes about her duties in a very professional manner. Her partner in crime deterrence also has to be certified to work in conjunction with the dog. It is a team relationship.

Scout owes her success to her partner who drives her around to crime scenes. Her prime asset is her superlative nose, which is a remarkable device for detecting the subtle aromas of a variety of drugs. There is literally no place to hide when Scout is on the scent and dope hidden inside upholstered chairs or inside plaster walls just does not escape her detection. Sometimes the stuff isn't there any more but Scout's nose can still trace the fact that it was once hidden within.

The life and career of a sniffer dog is often dangerous as drug dealers are prone to seek revenge when caught by Scout. Therefore, handlers take extra precautions to see to it that their canine charges are not put to undue risk.

Unfortunately, even with the best of care, working dogs such as Scout have a rather short working career. They suffer from burnout just as their humans counterparts do, but since their lifespan is shorter, so is their career frame. Their retirement years are apt to be golden ones however for no matter what else occurs, they endear themselves so deeply to their comrades, and especially their partner handlers, that there is no question about their golden futures.

This symbiotic relationship has been repeated time after time through the centuries since man and dog first befriended each other.

And the world is better for it.

WHY??

BIZARRE: Strikingly odd, as in manner of style; eccentric; grotesque.

Many times I am asked to relate the most unusual incident I have ever encountered in dealing with animals. That is not easy to do since numerous events are highly interesting but not at all unusual while others are highly unusual but scarcely interesting. But if substituting the word 'bizarre' for 'unusual,' one episode comes to mind above all others. As a matter of fact, it sounds like something Stephen King would create to excite, dismay and horrify. But it did happen, although gruesome, depressing, shocking, revolting and true.

AS MENTIONED PREVIOUSLY, there are presently a number of radio monitoring devices on the market that can tune in on various government agency transmissions. They are usually called scanners, and some are portable models which can be installed in vehicles. They can trace fire, sheriff, police and highway patrol transmissions. They can listen but they cannot broadcast.

These agencies know that private citizens do monitor their messages and that quite often the stuff is exciting, causing large crowds of onlookers to show up at some scene of action. The curious thus get in the way, obstruct and sometimes interfere with the agencies' rescue work. To alleviate to some extent such type of intrusion, those agencies will often say nothing at all about the reason for service requests, not even in code. The call I got for assistance was like that.

When I arrived at the nice little duplex on Biddle Street there were several marked cars there but no clues except that it was a police matter. It was the police who had called. The real clue came from the unmarked car bearing an exempt plate that was also present. It belonged to the coroner and that told me that bodies were involved.

I parked the van and asked the first uniformed officer I saw to point out the officer in charge. He told me to go on in since the rest of the guys were inside with the coroner.

The interior of the house was bare. There was no furniture to speak of and all the knickknacks, pictures, lamps and so on that indicate habitation were gone. Several neatly labeled moving boxes were stacked around in corners, out of the way. They were taped, labeled and ready to be moved or stored. It was strange.

The coroner came down the stairs at about that time and told me that my part was upstairs with the bodies. They hadn't moved anything yet so 'be prepared' was his advice. That warning was appreciated since I have been on calls involving the deceased when the police didn't clue me in as to the nature of the call and the results can be really unsettling.

But even knowing as much as I did beforehand, I was not ready for what I saw. I knew by that time that upstairs was a homicide-suicide case. I knew that there was an animal involved but at that juncture I merely contemplated a capture.

When I got to the top of the stairs I looked around the room and saw a woman lying on a pallet on the floor of the main bed-room. Again, there was literally no furniture. On one wall immediately to the left there was a tall dresser pushed up against a door which probably led to a bathroom. The lady on the floor was neatly attired in an attractive housecoat and bedroom slippers and had her hands crossed over her bosom. She was in the position usually associated with repose in a casket.

The oddity was the plastic bag over her head which prevented the blood from the bullet hole in her temple from messing up the floor. The situation was getting weirder by the minute.

Next to the lady was another neatly wrapped box with a double strand of packing string wrapped around it. A typewritten note was taped to the top of the box. The coroner told me that the box had a cat in it, according to the note, but that they hadn't opened it up yet. They wanted me to do that.

I nodded OK to that one but bothered to ask: Where was the other body? He looked at me with a funny expression on his face.

"Right there," he said, pointing to the dresser.

How could I have not noticed the body on the top of the dresser in front of the door that was probably a bathroom. Could it have been because it did not look like the body of a human being? It looked more like a mannikin. Not like the older ones with hair and eyes and facial features. It was more like the new modernistic ones that are made chalky white and without features that look more like space aliens than people.

The proof that the suicides had been well planned had already been obvious: The clean house, the stored furniture, the neatly packed and wrapped boxes of personal belongings and the tidy way that the female had been killed. She was obviously a willing participant for, after all, she did allow the plastic bag to be placed over her face and head in order not to soil the carpet.

But it was the male that presented the final proof of the plot. The killing weapon was a .22 caliber rifle. It is an easy gun to use to kill someone else but a bit more difficult to use as a suicide weapon as it cannot be placed at the temple as easily as a handgun.

Because of its long barrel, a shot with the muzzle-to-the-mouth method might not kill as the bullet might not hit the brain squarely enough. Plus, the small calibre does not do as much tissue damage as a larger calibre round would do. So, in order to assure that he would die, the gentleman had arranged an automatic hanging if the shot failed to do the job. And this was what made the scene so bizarre.

He had carefully measured a length of strong rope to be used. In the process he gave a new insight into the expression 'give him enough rope to hang himself.' He fashioned a proper hangman's noose on one end and then opened the door leading

WHY??

into the supposed bathroom. He placed the rope over the top of the door and allowed the loose end to fall to the floor. He then slipped the rope under the door and brought it up again, tying it securely to the knob. Next, he closed the door firmly so that it latched tightly. The rope was bound to some degree by the pressure exerted against it at both top and bottom and totally secured by tying it to the doorknob.

Only one thing was left to do and that was to secure the door itself in case the latch didn't hold and allowed the door to swing open and release the tension on the rope.

So, at this point he drove wooden wedges between the door frame and the door. The door thus could not be opened. He put the hammer away with the rest of the tools in a cardboard box and taped it shut, just like the rest of the boxes in the house. This was an incredibly neat person and one whose composure in the face of a soon-to-be-committed suicide was incredible.

He then climbed up onto the top of the tall dresser and secured the noose around his neck and shot himself. The autopsy revealed that the precautions were unnecessary. The bullet did the job and his body just hung from the rope instead of falling to the floor.

I opened the appointed box for which I was responsible. The cat had been lovely in life. It was a long-haired white male, probably an Angora. He had not been shot but had been hung and his rope and noose were still around his neck as he lay in death wrapped in baby blankets enclosed in a plastic bag inside the neatly wrapped box.

There were a lot of questions left unanswered. There was no suicide note and both of the people were in fair health. They were elderly, to be sure, but neither was suffering from disability or terminal illness, according to witnesses.

But strangest of all was the mystery of the cat. Why the cat?

A TALL ORDER

Serendipity. Isn't that a beautiful word? It sort of rolls off the tongue. And it takes on a special meaning, especially when it happens to you.

THE WHOLE EPISODE had to do with a big dog. Not just a big dog, but a REALLY BIG dog.

Large dogs are the nemesis of shelters everywhere. They are ever so much harder to place in adoptive homes than are the smaller varieties. The easiest ones to relocate are the toys, those tiny little fellows that fit nicely onto your lap and leave some lap left over.

The problems with larger dogs as adoption material are simple to enumerate. They eat too much. They can fill a whole car all by themselves and they can't learn how to drive it. Sometimes their wagging tail can strike you like an inquisitor's whip. And their droppings make you think an elephant has wandered through your yard.

Big dogs also break things in the house just getting from here to there. They have a bark that shatters eardrums, if not mirrors. And if they jump up on you unexpectedly, you go down for the count. Walking a big dog can be a marathon event all by itself. So large dogs worry us and we put extra effort into finding homes for them.

It was a Saturday morning when I found myself holding down the office and kennel while my companion officer handled field calls. It was past noon and the day had been disappointingly slow. Saturday is usually the best day for adoptions but this one was not working out like it was supposed to.

Then I heard a car door close and soon in walked a lady. She was young, mid-thirties perhaps, and well attired. If she were an adoption candidate at all, I figured maybe a Poodle type, something small, neat and well mannered. I had little on our roster to choose from in that category, so my optimism did not rise.

After the usual greetings and small talk, she informed me that she was interested in adopting a dog as a friend and companion. She wanted to know all about the process: adoption costs and related rules. Interestingly enough, she did not ask any questions about the breeds or types available for adoption. That is frequently one of the first questions people ask since they normally insist on a particular type dog if not a specific breed. Either that, or they want to go out to the compound first to see if anything catches their fancy. The details can always come later.

This lady did neither. She asked all about the rules first. I explained how the adoption program worked and how the requirements for spaying, neutering and licensing were to be met. I explained how all the dogs were handled in the same way, regardless of age, sex, species and so forth.

She countered with a few pertinent questions but never once gave any indication of what her preference might be. Soon she had the whole picture and I politely offered to show her the way to the shelter so that she could view what we had available for adoption that day.

"No thank you," she said. "I'll be leaving now."

Needless to say, I was struck dumb. After going through the whole procedure in detail, she was apparently just going to drop the whole idea. Dejected, I felt like the proverbial salesman who had spent the whole morning making his best pitch only to have the customer walk out.

It didn't fit. It wasn't consistent with everything that we had been reviewing ever since she arrived. I, being not overly bashful but considerably confused, asked her why she was not going to follow through by at least looking around the kennel. Or, to put it another way, why did she come here in the first place?

Her reasons were quickly explained. She really wanted a dog and she really liked dogs, all kinds. However, dogs are a serious responsibility. She was willing to accept that but only if she could find the one dog on which she had her heart set. Since dog pounds never seemed to have her kind of dog, she just couldn't bear to go out and look at all the others waiting anxiously for someone to love them enough to take them home. She knew that she was not going to adopt just anything and it would make her feel guilty to look at them knowing that. It was an intriguing viewpoint and not an unreasonable one.

We always welcome people who really seriously want to adopt and accept responsibilities toward the pet they select. So, her reaction was at least consistent with our desires. However, I was not yet satisfied. I could not imagine what kind of dog she could possibly want that never shows up in kennels. Given enough time, we almost always get just about every breed of canine ever created.

So, I asked. It turns out that she wants a Great Dane. I'll have to admit that Danes are not a common dog to have in a shelter, especially in ranch country. And now that my interest was thoroughly captured, I inquired whether she would be more interested in a male or female. I figured that as long as she was going to walk out anyway, I might as well play out the game to the end. It turns out she wanted a female Great Dane, adult variety, no puppies please.

I pointed out that this was an unusual order but that one thing was still missing from her list. What color would she like this wonder dog to be. Yep. Of course the most difficult of colors to obtain in that particular breed: the Harlequin.

Well, I had been with the Department over eight years during which we had only had a mere half dozen Danes in residence. The encounter that Saturday may sound like a tale as tall as the dog, but can you imagine the long arm of coincidence?

Back in the outer reaches of the shelter that day was the only Harlequin Great Dane that had been in our kennel since my association with it. Eight years, one lady, one dog. Maybe there is such a thing as Divine Intervention. Serendipity!

A WALK IN THE PARK

ASK JUST ABOUT ANY SCIENTIST what the first truly significant invention in history was and he will likely tell you that it was the advent of the wheel. Some will no doubt give top ranking to fire, which was not an invention but a discovery, while others will give priority to the stone axe or the Archimedes screw. But for many of the peoples who originated in the vast frozen reaches of the Far Northlands, a strip of wood was the likely candidate.

If you take this long strip of wood and turn one end up slightly, you will have invented a runner. If you do a couple of them and tie them onto your feet, you will have discovered skis. Now if you are really ingenious and bind a pair of them in parallel with a little space in between, then secure it all up in cured animal skins, you have invented the sled. So far so good.

But, if you add a brace of dogs you have invented the dog sled which was, for aeons, the finest conveyance available for the frozen land of the Far North. The problem was: you cannot invent a dog.

Well, God can and he did it, in spades. Out of the Arctic regions came a dog so superbly suited for the job that no others need apply. In his native land it had been bred for some 3,000 years, give or take a hundred, and is known as the Chukchi, after the local tribe that God blessed first with this animal. He is known to them as the dog that, in either work or play, can outdistance all the others.

We have known this dog as the Siberian Husky ever since it was first introduced into the United States by natives of the Chukchi Seacoast north of the Bering Sea early in the 1900s. We have to agree with the Chukchis. He is indefatigable and is literally without peer in endurance and stamina. When at work in his natural environment, he can pull a sled from sunup to sundown with such joyous abandon as to be second cousin to perpetual motion for he is a self-sustaining engine.

Inbred in the process is the dog's need to roam and run. Nevada and Arizona would be adequate for an afternoon's spin. It was this heritage that spelled trouble for one Siberian.

Four o'clock in the morning normally means absolutely nothing to a dog. They are not given to clock-watching. But at four o'clock in the morning when the bakery across the street fired up its fryer and started the day's bake, the aroma was enough to drive a guy nuts. Furthermore, if you nudge this little metal bar thing just right, the gate would swing wide open and a fella could go over there and panhandle.

The first time we picked up the black and white Husky there, we booked him into doggy jail and his owners came in and bailed him out.

It was only a week later that we encountered him at the donut shop again. This time, we were the good guys and we stuck him back into his yard with a warning note to his owners.

That didn't work either and so we had to impound him once more a few days later. Talk about wanderlust. The next time the dog came into the center was his last. The owner declined to reclaim.

Oh no. It wasn't the last for the Husky. We placed the dog into a new home in just a day or two after its owners renounced all claim. He was adopted on Thursday afternoon, taken home, fed, cleaned, loved and renamed Sierra. He settled into his new place and didn't seem to miss the donut shop at all.

However, his lust for travel, adventure and new places soon overcame his common sense and Sierra was off and running again. It didn't take long for he left home Friday afternoon.

We at Animal Control are experienced at this sort of thing and we soon had all of the bases covered. If the dog showed up anywhere, we would likely hear of it. We had pulled out all the stops to find Sierra because this was one of our own, so to speak.

By midday on Saturday we had a report of a Husky running the pastures at Jack's Valley Road and the dog answered the description of Sierra. However, in the 24 hours that he had been on the lam, the distance from his new home and where he was now reported encompassed a span of at least 25 miles, and not as the crow flies either.

The route had taken him partly through town and partly over the low mountain foothills through a combined dairy and bison ranch. Where he had been most recently seen was in Genoa, one of the earliest settlements in the Nevada Territory. It had to be a look-alike dog. Sierra couldn't have traveled that far in such a short time. Still....

By Sunday morning there had been no further suspicious sightings and Sierra had not come home on his own. There was little doubt that he could find his way home should he be so inclined. They read maps, you know. The uncertainty, the not knowing, the unanswered, compelled the new owners to drive to the Hot Springs where a Husky had last been seen.

Since most stories have happy endings, this cannot be an exception. When we responded, we found that the dog was, indeed, Sierra. But, amazingly, he wasn't even tired. Twenty-five miles to a Husky is just a mere walk in the park!

WILD HORSES
OF THE GREAT BASIN

*A noted storyteller and sometime historian, Rufus
Steele, wrote eloquently of the wild horses known
as the Mustangs long before Ford Motor Company
ever borrowed the term.*

*Steele spoke of his work as fact-fiction and his
words wove a tapestry of real-west folklore,
coupled with an appreciation for the wild horse.
He summed it up best when he said, in effect,
that the person who does not love a horse is a
person who needs pity or help.*

LEGENDS ABOUND on the life
and times of the wild horse herds
of the west and the men who set
out to capture and tame them.
Charles 'Pete' Barnum was one
such horse trapper, or mustanger,
of such renown that he was known as the king of the rangemen.
Horses to match the stature of the men who pursued them rose
to equal fame. The hunter and the hunted were to stand in
history as equals.

One such stallion was named Scar Neck, after a wound
inflicted by Shoshone hunters. Only exceptional horses were given
names and the simple act of being recognized and named was a
sign of excellence. Scar Neck spent his life evading the best capture techniques that both the white hunters and the Shoshone
Indians could devise. He roamed the desert in freedom until
natural death overtook him.

Only when the concept of capture gave way to the concept of
slaughter did the horse become truly threatened. A stallion is

simply no match for a bullet. Still, the wild horse hangs tenaciously to life and the rangeland is both vast and filled with hiding places for the wily Mustang. So vast are the lands of the Great Basin that the horse herds flourished in spite of man, living and growing in places so remote that rarely, if ever, was man to trod upon his land. So the Mustang lives on.

Throughout most of history, the horse has played a pivotal role and is deemed the most valuable animal that man has domesticated. Prior to the invention of the automobile, the horse performed the chores of transport from individual use in agriculture to being the forerunner of the tractor and even the railroads.

It was likewise the stalwart of warfare cavalry, replaced only by tanks and trucks. The number of horses in the United States reached its highest level around 1918 when it was reported that there were more than twenty million horses on farms in the U.S. By the early 1960s, the U.S. Department of Agriculture reported that figure had dwindled to about three million.

But the horse dates back some fifty million years. The ancient horse was said to resemble the horse as we know it today but was reputedly only about one foot high. That horse, which scientists called *Eohippus*, appeared at about the same time in both Europe and America.

It had no horns or claws with which to protect itself, so it developed speed as its weapon. It grew in size and weight but mysteriously died out in Europe. The American horse however, gradually spread to Asia across the land bridge that supposedly once connected the two continents at Alaska.

Then the American horse reputedly died out too. Archaeologists have found equine remains, together with other relics in caves but the first record of the horse as a domestic animal dates back prior to 2500 B.C. This initial taming occurred in Asia and was found so useful that the tamed horse soon became common in Europe, most of Asia and parts of Africa.

The first important use of horses appears to have been in warfare, hitched to chariots and later used as cavalry mounts. It was the horse that made possible the conquests of Alexander the Great and Genghis Khan.

As the centuries passed, the horse was used for both work and sports and soon became a status symbol of high rank or wealth.

It was the Spanish who returned the horse to America after it had disappeared centuries before. While North American Natives are associated with fine horses, they actually only inherited them from the Spanish who came to the New World and brought their horses with them. When they left, they preferred to load their ships with gold and silver, and thus set their horses free. Those steeds ran wild over North and South America and today so do their descendants, the Mustangs.

Presently, much of the wild horse population lies within the borders of the State of Nevada in the Great Basin area. Likewise, much of the wild horse population known as Mustangs roams within this state. We who are privileged to live here often see small bands of Mustangs on the sage-covered hills. There is a certain magnificence to the wild horse and to be in its presence is to share in that glory. There is also a sense of awe and a union of spiritual freedom which a herd invariably inspires in the human viewer.

But that peaceful union was shattered on a clear, cold spring day several years ago, when a report came in that a herd of Mustangs roaming the Pinion Hills at the edge of Carson City had been slaughtered at the hands of man—shot and dropped as they grazed on the spring grasses of the foothills. They had not even sensed the presence of danger. They had grazed there for several summers in perfect peace, but not this time.

We counted seven of them: one magnificent white stallion that was the favorite of Mustang aficionados everywhere, five mares and two yearlings. The killer was no respecter of either sex or age. All were fair marks for the heavy bullets fired by the big game rifle used for the killings.

My supervisor is much more of an expert on firearms than I am. Perhaps that is why he is the supervisor and I am the officer. He offered a preliminary opinion that the weapon would prove to be an old-fashioned large caliber gun often used for big game such as elk and buffalo. It would develop that he was right on target in that opinion.

There is an ongoing argument in Nevada as to who has jurisdiction over the wild horse herds. Most often the federal agency known as the Bureau of Land Management is recognized as the responsible entity.

But the BLM, as it is known, often denies that jurisdiction on the grounds that the present-day horse is not a true hammerhead Mustang, which is the only horse for which that bureau is responsible. All other horses are considered as previously owned animals, such as used cars are previously owned, and thus are outside the purview of BLM.

They claim that most of the Nevada herds fall under this distinction and are simply horses that people have dumped in the desert because they no longer wanted them. The result is that nobody accepts responsibility for them. So, inasmuch as the shootings occurred in our jurisdiction, we stepped in and took over.

My supervisor and I walked the foothills for hours, taking photos and notes on the horses found dead. There could have been others farther away. There was no way to know as the hills are huge and much of the area is not accessible except by foot. We agreed that the horses were apparently all shot with a heavy caliber gun and that most likely the same gun was used on all of the slain steeds.

I explored the possibility that one of the ranchers had shot the Mustangs since those herds often confiscated great quantities of ranchers' hay which was stockpiled for winter use. But I ultimately stood both corrected and apologetic. The theory had only seemed reasonable.

We never learned what really happened and I hate to sound conspiratorial but the investigation simply fizzled. It slowed, stalled, and finally died and no one was ever formally charged. We hoped that the investigation got close enough to somebody that it scared him—or anyone else—from ever repeating such a dastardly deed. But we were wrong.

As recently as the last week of December, 1998, 33 beautiful wild horses—stallions, mares, pregnant mares and mares with new foals—were again found both maimed and slaughtered in

Lagomarsino and Devil's Flat Canyons of the Virginia Range outside Reno, Nevada, leaving both residents and officers shocked and enraged.

Three youths have since been arrested and charged (although as of this writing, they have not yet been tried). We understand the incident gained national attention, leaving the population in general aghast at the mentality that would so senselessly harm innocent animals that are so much a part of the Nevada landscape.

Nevada has been termed a wasteland by some not stalwart enough to trod its soil. But those of us who live here know that beneath the magnificent canopy of open sky lies a rich and fertile land. And there is no more noble beast to serve as symbol of this free and open space than the wild horse of the Great Basin.

The beauty of a Mustang standing guard on a hill, wind-whipped and proud, speaks well for the spirit of this area for those who have the will to see it. Hail to the Mustang. May we forever share this land with you!

"So when do we get to the part
where the he kisses the horse?"

ODDBALLS

CAPYBARA: "Native to banks and streams in South America, resembling a large guinea pig, the largest living rodent." So says my MacMillan dictionary. Ha! Fat lot they know. They've never been to Akron, Ohio, that's for sure. Being a native Buckeye, I can proudly boast that nobody raises bigger and better rats than Ohio, MacMillan to the contrary.

THERE IS A CANAL that goes through Akron, a waterway which was built a long time before I was born. It was designed, so they say, to carry freight barges from lake to lake, of which Ohio has an abundance. The canal went past the loading docks of a cereal company which had been built on the banks of the canal so that the barges could be unloaded right at the plant's docks.

And that's what attracted rats. Most people feel pretty much repulsed by rats. They are the ultimate yuck animal. And with good reason.

I can remember when I was just a kid. We would walk the full length of the Canal from where it passed a familiar landmark to where the cereal docks were located. Rail lines had long since replaced the barges. When the waterway was replaced by the railway, the lines were elevated over the canal. Tons of cereal were spilled in the unloading process and this made for a pigeon haven. And rats. Big rats.

If you have never seen one of those huge river rats, you have missed one of the most chilling sights your eyes could ever behold. I mean, these guys are BIG. And hairy. And somehow slimy too. No cat in its right mind would ever even think of attacking one of those monsters. They were twice as big as the average large cat. They had dirty yellow eyes that glowed in the dark, plus teeth like beavers.

No one in that area ever, not ever, went into a dark area without a good flashlight as those rats were without fear. They had none of the furtiveness usually associated with rodents. They would walk right over your feet if you were foolish enough to stand still when they were around.

I never stood still around them. One time I picked up a couple of rocks and lobbed one at a large rat wobbling along a path in front of me. Fortunately for me, I missed, but the sound of the rock made the rat pause and turn to glare at me. I put the other rock down gently and said, "Sorry" and stole away.

With this as background, you can imagine how well I appreciated the panic in the lady's voice.

The call came in when I was on graveyard duty. You would think that rats would not be allowed in such an influential neighborhood, but there he was. The lady informed me that she had a sopping wet rat trapped in her bathroom and I jolly well better get myself down there on the double and remove it. The rat, it seemed, had come up through the sewer line, swam through the trap and emerged wet but happy out of the commode. It is rare, but it can be done. She nearly coronaried when she opened the door to confront a slimy wet rat in the toilet bowl.

It only took a couple of minutes to capture and remove the intruder but I'll bet it took a lot longer for the lady to feel comfortable again in her own bathroom. Betcha she kept the lid down!

FOR ANOTHER FUN JOB, try cutting a Pit Bull loose from a barbed wire fence in which he had become thoroughly enmeshed, tangled, snarled and otherwise entwined.

It seems that several strands of old rusty wire pinned this fellow to the ground after he tried to tunnel under the wood fence that bordered his property. Little did he know there was an older rusty wire fence beyond. His frantic efforts to free himself simply wound one or more of the wires around his body until he could barely move without getting jabbed.

It was about that time that he decided to quit struggling and simply lie back and assess the situation. It was also about that time that Zach and I showed up in response to a call from the dog's neighbor. We looked him over from head to toe, front to back and tried to decide how and where to start cutting.

Zach prudently suggested we start at the end that didn't have teeth and I was forced to agree. The Pit just stared at us with his gold-hued eyes, showing neither aggression nor friendship.

Know what? It was a piece of cake. We just continued to cut from the rear toward his mouth while holding his head down. Some of the barbs must have stung when they were snipped out but Pit Bulls are tough. It's called gameness. In fact, I once knew a Pit that frolicked around for several hours with a hunting knife broken off at the hilt and stuck in his chest. Once the knife was removed, the Pit went on about his business as though nothing had happened. So it was with this guy. When we finished cutting, he scrambled under the fence and back into the safety of his own yard where he put on an exhibition of joyous abandon. Zach and I both thought he was duly grateful.

LIFE IS LIKE THAT IN ANIMAL CONTROL. Day after day without anything of note, and then something happens that becomes one for the book. If you think cutting a Pit Bull loose from a barbed wire fence is tough, try hog-tying a deer. It is not an easy thing to do since the deer is no more cooperative than any other frightened animal and is considerably more unruly. A number of Animal Control, as well as Wildlife Officers, have tried to save injured deer, which seem to be a fragile lot as wild animals go, and many of the efforts to rescue them have come to naught.

The call came in from an upscale woodsy suburb. A deer had become entangled in a partially downed barbed wire fence. Several of the wire strands were on the ground but the one still up on the posts was enough to bring the deer down. It was not clear what injury it had sustained. He was just prone and frightened but his legs did not seem to be broken. There was no blood visible, and no open wounds on his body. Perhaps it was a neck or spinal injury that kept him there. But he did not seem to have any problem in trying to hook me with his antlers. His watchful eyes followed my every movement.

The couple who phoned in the incident stood by to assist but they were not able to shed any light on what had befallen the deer. He was down when they found him and since they had been working in the yard all day long, except for an occasional iced tea break, he could not have been there very long. Whatever happened had occurred just a few minutes before they discovered it.

Incidentally, 'yard' is misleading relative to the property in that section of town. The yard not only included the lawn and other landscaped areas, it also encompassed the surrounding virgin woods. It was an area of tall pines as well as sagebrush since it was in the foothills of the Sierra.

There is never enough money, it seems, to go around in care of wild animals. Economists call it scarce resources but it always means the same thing under any other title. There is no such thing as a free lunch. Veterinarians need to be paid, not only for their time but also for the consumption of expensive medication used during treatment. Likewise, Animal Controls, Humane Societies and Fish and Game Departments do not have budgets large enough to treat wildlife in general for medical emergencies. Therefore the answer, poor as it might be, is to be very selective about which animals and what type injuries receive treatment.

Deer are high on the priority list of favored species and since this fella, although obviously injured, did not seem to be beyond redemption, I was able to find in his favor. That meant that he had to be transported in some fashion and that is easier said than done.

I grasped one leg and slipped a rope around it while he kicked me with the other leg. I caught that leg as well and he promptly hooked me with a horn. I grabbed a horn and snagged a leg to it and he grew a couple more legs to kick me again. It was a question of whether I would run out of rope before he ran out of legs, but I got there first. He gave a new meaning to the term 'tie the knot' but the job was finally completed. He did give me a final swat with his tail when he ran out of legs just to show me his disdain.

Once the hooking and kicking were over, I solicited some help from the standbys and we loaded the deer onto a stretcher and into the van.

Hot, tired, sweaty and only a little bloody, we took off for the Vet's. Unfortunately, the deer had expired by the time it arrived there. No autopsy was performed but presumably trauma played a part in its demise as deer are extremely sensitive and panic easily.

If Animal Control Officers could just wave a magic wand!

"Me? When I grow up I want to be a silk purse."

INTERLUDE

IT WAS A DARK AND STORMY NIGHT, Snoopy's eternally futile efforts to write the great American novel notwithstanding. And it was definitely one of those nights in Carson City, a capital that normally enjoys an unending expanse of sparkling night sky vistas extending beyond the towering tips of the Sierra and the other lesser ranges that surround the flatlanders who dwell on the valley floor. But not this night.

The usual star-dimpled sky was an unbroken mass of gunbarrel black with nary a suggestion of a twinkle anywhere. The rising moon gave up its struggle to subdue the impenetrable thunderclouds that stubbornly refused to offer any hint of remission. Soon, each giant raindrop soaked up its share of the limited light cast by street lamps that were, by contrast, merely dim blobs against the intermittent bolts of fierce lightning that permeated the area, leaving in their wake a foreboding gloom. It was indeed a dark and stormy night.

I had been summoned to venture forth into this wet mess via a phone call from the Sheriff's office, our off-duty dispatch agency. They had received a telephone call from a motorist driving down Curry Street. At least he had been driving. Now he was in the comfort of his own home. He reported that he had seen something lying in the rain-filled gutter next to the road. He thought that it might have been a small animal there but he wasn't sure since it was so dark, what with the unrelenting rain descending in sheets. The motorist was, after all, not an official person who gets paid to get wet. So he elected to stay in his car and guess at what might have been in the gutter. And he guessed it might be a dog lying there. Or, it could have been a plastic trash bag. He was uncertain.

We, on the other hand, are not paid to guess. We are paid to validate first and then react accordingly. So I soon found myself cruising the darkness of Curry Street looking for a lump of blackness which was darker than the rest of the night around it. While there might indeed be a dog out there, I was not counting on it. Rain, combined with dark and shiny wet roadways, can play tricks on the mind's eye and I sorta figured this was one of those cases.

So to save time in the driving rain, I had taken off in my personal car instead of going to the Shelter for a more official ultramodern fully-equipped Animal Control vehicle. (Read that: Dodge van with a couple of dog leashes, a blanket and other rescue accoutrements.)

I completed a north-to-south pass to no avail and then reversed the course for a south-to-north search. This too, was soon accomplished with the same unsatisfying results. It was time to get out and get wet.

I was soaking up my second gallon of water when, thanks to a flash of lightning, I spotted the little guy in the gutter. He appeared to be lifeless. Was I too late? Had rain and shock completed the job that rubber and steel had started?

I stooped low and gathered up the drenched little critter in my hands. He was a tinymite and fit nicely there. But his head drooped limply off to one side. Just as I deemed that I was indeed too late for this one, a small tremor worked its way through his little body. Life still clung there. Was it enough?

Now I wished that I had followed the rules and taken a van. Dogcatchers don't really need a lot of equipment and I was being a bit facetious about my ultramodern vehicle but, vans do have radios and had I taken a van, I could have called in an alert to the veterinary hospital. They would then know that I was coming and most importantly, I would know that they were in fact there and on duty. But no, I had blown that option. Now it was 'wing and a prayer' time. It was possible that, due to the lateness of the hour, the on-duty Doc would be upstairs in his apartment, sound asleep. If so, I would have the devil's own time getting him up without that van alert.

Fortunately, after blowing my car horn, beating on the door with my nightstick, and a lot of vocalizing, I got the good Doc's attention. An hour later I was on my way back home and the little black guy was holding his own. He had shots and intravenous fluids dripping into his veins, was curled up under a heating pad and was recipient of such other stuff as deemed necessary for his survival. He would make it A-OK.

Rain-soaked and shivering, I resorted that night to my favorite antidote for such situations: a senior citizen's discount on coffee at a major fast-food emporium. I don't mind having to admit I qualify. I even ask for it. And I go inside for my big bargain as I don't like drive-thru windows and their attendant raspy loud-speakers.

Tempus fugits, as it is prone to do. Then one night ten thousand coffees later while I was again on my way out of the golden arches with my favorite discounted brew, a gentleman sitting in the far corner got up from his chair and gestured to me. As I approached, he extended his hand and I returned the prof-fered handshake without knowing why. He cleared that up.

"I have wanted for a long time to thank you in person for the service you rendered for me. You saved my little dog's life nearly five years ago. I'll never forget it, or you, for doing that. And do you know what impressed me the most? You did it using your own private car!"

So this was the gent who had thanked me so profusely via a letter-to-the-editor of the local newspaper the day following that rescue five years earlier!

Although such an accolade is one of the much-appreciated perks of the job, the gent obviously felt so grateful about the incident I couldn't tell him it was my mistake and that I was in error in using my own car. How do you admit that stupidity spawned a reluctant hero?

ONLY YOU....

AT FIRST GLANCE it resembles a piece of junk beside the highway. Then it moves, and it becomes a ball of fur, once well groomed, but now disheveled, dirty and full of burrs.

At the approach of every car it has a dual reaction: one to run in fright, the other to linger, hoping perhaps, to once again hear the familiar roar of its beloved owner's car.

But that will never happen because that thoughtless travesty of humanity is too selfish to make certain the unwanted little dog has a new home. Instead, it is easier to just abandon it along some highway, leaving the frightened, hungry and thirsty former pet to fend for itself. Too often, in its panic, it becomes road kill.

But you can change all that. The easy solution is to take the critter to the nearest animal shelter for possible adoption. But there the little waif will meet a couple dozen others just like himself, homeless, of mixed breed because no one bothered to have his predecessors spayed or neutered, hence it is now a fit candidate for the dreaded euthanasia chamber.

What does it take to impress you, and you, and you that more responsibility must be assumed to make certain all those unwanted canine or feline pregnancies never occur, that no more trusting, friendly little pets meet certain death at the shelter because no one cared?

Granted a 'no kill' compound is a marvelous idea, but in reality, it is only an idea that is, hopefully, spreading. For starters, the Reno (Nevada) Society for the Prevention of Cruelty to Animals

(SPCA), in early 1999, initiated a new adoption and thrift center, which facility offers rescued and homeless animals for adoption.

The center's plans likewise include services for a low-cost spay/neuter clinic, the ultimate goal being a "no kill" community allowing more pets to be saved and adopted. The facility utilizes the services of volunteers, as well as donations. The founders are hoping the operation will be a model and a challenge to other communities to emulate their program.

There is also the noteworthy plan sponsored by SPAY/USA that helps people locate veterinarians or programs with affordable spay/neuter services for cats and dogs. The organization is making a special effort to reach people who resist or procrastinate in getting their pets to the vet to be spayed, neutered and vaccinated.

The organization is attempting to reach the hard-core resistant one percent of the populace that results in the killing of six million surplus cats and dogs annually. Their campaign is called STOP (Start Targeting One-Percenters). Their counselors also offer information on the nearest participating veterinarian, clinic or program that offers low-cost spay/neuter programs.

Whether we like it or not, euthanasia is an indispensable component of animal control. It represents the dark and ugly side of the rescue effort and it matters little if the agency doing it is an institution operated by a governing agency or by an independent humane society.

The end result, the bottom line, is that due to lack of funds, hence facilities, death is the ultimate solution to many of the problems encountered in animal control. The resolution rests with you and all the others out there who object to the death sentence for those little tail-waggers that wait so desperately to be loved. Truth is truth and no one bemoans the euthanasia truth more than those who must implement it.

The early 1900s ushered in a movement for the more humane treatment of pets although many of the ideas met with great resistance. For example, would you believe, in that emerging era, many considered it a waste of time and compassion to worry about the lifestyle of dogs and cats? There were few, however, who would begrudge even an animal the dignity of a painless death.

The scientific solution to the pet overpopulation has not yet been adequately explored even though the idea is publicized. Other than spay, a truly proactive approach to the problem rather than a reactive one has yet to be implemented. Strict birth control measures would certainly be welcomed by animal control officers, particularly those who must, unfortunately, 'man the needles' or 'push the buttons.'

So to all of you out there: Join *The Price is Right* TV game-show host Bob Barker and spread the word. "Help control the pet population. Have your pet spayed or neutered." Only you can guarantee that those heart-tugging, abandoned pets lining up at the shelter fence just waiting to be adopted, will live to their own cycle of ripe old age replete with the joy they're capable of spreading. It is *YOU* who must inject the 'control' into animal control. Only *you* can make it happen!

ABOUT THE AUTHOR

BORN AND REARED in what was once known as the Rubber City, Akron, Ohio, in a conventional family setting of the low-key '30s and '40s, the author says he lived an undistinguished childhood, along with his brother and sister. Highlight of those early years was a dog or two.

Following high school graduation, counselors and aptitude testing indicated a strong propensity toward the more cerebral professions such as accounting, law or social work.

Thus so guided, he gained his accounting credentials but found the category did not deliver the promised euphoria. Then the exigencies of the Korean War headed him in a different direction. He sat out the conflict in Salzburg, Austria, serving as company clerk, thus avoiding the more onerous segments of military life such as guard duty and KP.

Returning from service, he rejoined the commercial world, holding down uninspired but stable positions in various business endeavors. In spare time he also tackled law studies. That too did not hold up to its blissful prognostications so he just continued working at dull, uninspiring positions, viewing further aptitude tests askance.

That's when Fate intervened and he found himself enthusiastic for the first time at the prospect of a change in career direction, that of Animal Control. It had been there, nagging at him all along. Why did it take him so long to recognize it?

Today, after a couple of decades in the Service, he is well known in the Great Basin for his soft-hearted approach to all God's creatures, great and small, coaxing even the most noxious into submission. He has even been known to stop traffic in order to rescue a hapless tortoise that, like the proverbial chicken, attempted to buck the odds and cross a busy highway.

Noted for his sunny disposition, keen sense of humor and affable demeanor, he was finally persuaded to record some of his many adventures and misadventures with critters.

Small wonder the byword during animal emergencies in the Great Basin was "Call Lee Wittek!"

EPILOGUE

Sadly, in the quiet of night on March 18, 1999, EVERETT LEE WITTEK, Carson City's popular Animal Control Officer, lost his battle with cancer. Fortunately, prior to his demise, Lee had the pleasure of reviewing the galley proofs of this, his first book delineating his various encounters with animals that crossed his path.

But this is only the beginning, as for quite some time, in earlier spare moments, he had been 'scribbling,' as he called it, recounting animal tales of countless friends who turned to him for advice and solace regarding their pets. That's when he let his imagination run wild, giving him impossible dreams of the big compound he envisioned to accommodate all the world's precious, abandoned strays he longed to befriend, each with a wagging tail that begged only a pat on the head and a scrap of food.

His sly, humorous, sometimes guarded words, attest to the fact Lee was a prolific writer whose talents and compassionate affinity for animals overflowed into his bulging journals left behind for all of us to enjoy.

We'll never forget you, Lee, and will always remember you for your infectious smile and mischievous grin...for your ability to shatter catastrophe with a humorous counterpoint...for your ready wit that camouflaged intense pain...and for your compassion toward every scroungy, homeless little mutt that shared your love, if only so briefly. Adios!

ABOUT THE AUTHOR